Lizzie ♥ Ethan

STRAPPED FOR CA$H

LIZZIE MCGUIRE
2-IN-1

EGMONT

EGMONT

We bring stories to life

Lizzie ♥ Ethan and *Strapped For Cash*
first published in the USA 2003
by Disney Press
First published in Great Britain 2004 by Egmont Books Limited
This edition first published 2005 by Egmont Books Limited
239 Kensington High Street, London, W8 6SA

Published by arrangement with Disney Press,
114 Fifth Avenue, New York, New York 10011-5690

ISBN 1 4052 2263 8

1 3 5 7 9 10 8 6 4 2

A CIP catalogue record for this title is available from the British Library

Printed and bound in Australia by Griffin Press

Adapted by Jasmine Jones
Based on the series created by Terri Minsky
Part one is based on a teleplay written
by Doug Tuber and Tim Maile.
Part two is based on a teleplay written
by Doug Tuber and Tim Maile.

EGMONT

Lizzie McGUiRE

PART ONE

CHAPTER ONE

"**P**udding cup!" David "Gordo" Gordon called. He was standing on a table in the middle of the crowded lunch patio, holding his dessert over his head. "Sealed! Untouched by cafeteria-lady hands! No skin! Do I hear one dollar?" A kid at a nearby table lifted his spoon in the air. "I've got a dollar." Gordo continued. "Do I hear one twenty-five?"

Lizzie McGuire and Miranda Sanchez walked over to Gordo's table, carrying their lunch trays. They stood there, staring up at him for a minute. "Gordo, why are you auctioning off your lunch?" Lizzie demanded.

"I need to make money for a new stereo," Gordo explained.

Miranda scrunched up her face and glanced at Lizzie. The friends looked up at Gordo dubiously. He didn't step down from the table, or even lower his pudding cup.

"What about your old stereo?" Lizzie wanted to know.

"It's gone to stereo heaven," Gordo said. Suddenly, he caught a flash of movement out of the corner of his eye. "You in the striped shirt!" he called. "One fifty for the pudding cup?" A kid in a green-yellow-and-black-striped jersey nodded and walked over. "One fifty. Going once, twice, sold! To the boy in the striped shirt." The kid passed Gordo a fistful of change, and Gordo handed over his prized pudding cup.

"So why don't you get your parents to buy you a new one?" Miranda said. Lizzie guessed her friend was talking about the stereo, not the pudding cup.

"That would be the logical answer," Gordo said as he climbed down from the table. "But my parents want me to earn the money on my own."

Gordo slid into a chair, and Miranda and Lizzie plopped their trays on the table and sat down across from him.

"I hate it when they say stuff like that!" Lizzie said as she settled her mesh bag with the big flower onto the ground next to her. Seriously. Just two days before, when they were in the drugstore, Lizzie's mom had actually said that Lizzie had plenty of lip gloss, and that if she wanted a new color, she should pay for it herself. As if lip gloss were something you could ever have "plenty" of! Parents.

"So, by brown-bagging my lunch and auctioning off my desserts, I can make about three dollars a day," Gordo explained. He looked down at his juice box dejectedly. "So I'll have a new stereo in five months."

Miranda, who had just popped a fry into her mouth, stopped midchew and had to swallow fast. "Five *months*?" she asked.

Gordo nodded. "Well, if you figure three dollars a day, five days a week—that's fifteen dollars," he explained. "And there are four weeks in a month, so that would be sixty dollars."

Miranda curled her lip and thought a minute, trying to follow the math.

"So, I'll have three hundred dollars in five months," Gordo finished.

"Wow, Gordo," Lizzie said, rolling her eyes. "Where were you during the math test today?"

"I was, uh," Gordo blew on his fingernails and rubbed them against his shirt, "getting my usual A."

Miranda and Lizzie looked at each other.

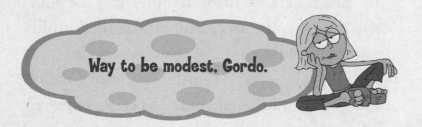

Way to be modest, Gordo.

"Well, if you're so smart, Mr. A," Lizzie said, giving him another eyeball roll, "you should already know how to raise money for your new stereo."

Gordo frowned. "What are you talking about?"

"Tutor math," Lizzie said, as if it were the most obvious thing in the world.

"People would totally pay for your help," Miranda chimed in.

"Oh, that's actually not a bad idea." Gordo pressed his lips together and nodded.

"Of course, it's not a bad idea." Lizzie tossed her hair and smiled. "*I* came up with it." She took a sip from her juice box. Besides, she thought, tutoring had to beat the humiliation of holding a daily pudding auction.

"Okay, I'll do it," Gordo said with finality. His eyes wandered over to the edge of Miranda's tray. "So, Miranda, how about a bite of that cupcake?"

Miranda picked up her cupcake and held it out toward Gordo. "Sure," she said.

Gordo grinned and reached for the cupcake, but Miranda pulled it back.

"For a buck fifty," Miranda told him with a crafty smile.

Gordo glowered at her, which only made Lizzie laugh. So much for Gordo's brilliant moneymaking scheme!

* * *

"Hey, Gordo," Lizzie said as she and Miranda walked into English class the next afternoon, "how many people have signed up for the tutoring?" The friends slipped into the two desks closest to Gordo, and Miranda smiled at him expectantly.

Gordo played with his pen. "Well, let's see . . . between that mad rush before school and the mob scene after first period?" He thought for a minute. "Zero."

Miranda's smile froze on her face. "Nobody's signed up yet?"

"No one," Gordo said. He dug around in his binder. "I even made these flyers."

Lizzie reached for the flyer. "Let me see that." She glanced down at the piece of paper. It looked like a chicken had crawled over it, trying to scratch a worm out of the paper.

How can anybody read this? Cave paintings are easier to understand.

Miranda grimaced at the flyer. "Is this in English?" Miranda asked.

Gordo frowned at her.

Lizzie's eyebrows drew together. "Who in their right mind would respond to something like this?"

At that very moment, Ethan—hottie of this and every single year, past and present—walked into class, carrying a piece of paper. "So, Gordon," he said, holding out a copy of Gordo's flyer, "is this you?"

"Yeah," Gordo said, clearly completely uninterested in anything Ethan had to say. Gordo glanced down at his notebook. "Yeah, it is."

Miranda's mouth fell open, and she glanced over at Lizzie. Lizzie had to press her lips together to keep from grinning like an idiot. Superhot Ethan needed a tutor! How lucky could she get? She and Miranda were practically Gordo's assistant tutors, right? After all, Lizzie had come up with the whole tutoring concept herself. They'd definitely get to hang with—er—*help* Ethan!

"So, you, like, uh, tutor math and stuff, right?" Ethan asked Gordo.

"Yeah, I do." Gordo looked at the paper in Ethan's hand and shook his head, as though he couldn't believe anyone had actually had trouble understanding his gorgeous flyer.

Ethan whipped out another piece of paper. "See, I kind of flagged the last test," he explained as he handed the exam over to Gordo, "and my 'rents think I could use some help."

Gordo frowned down at the test, like he didn't quite know what to do with it. Lizzie guessed that Mr. A had probably never seen a test with that much red on it before in his life.

The moment dragged on, and Lizzie's eyes bugged out. Why wasn't Gordo trying to sell himself as Ethan's tutor? Did he truly not grasp that this was a golden opportunity to hang out with the cutest guy in the known universe? Okay, it was true, Gordo was a guy. But couldn't he see what kind of an opportunity this was for Lizzie and Miranda? Lizzie snapped her fingers at Gordo. He looked up, and Lizzie pointed at Ethan.

Gordo looked confused. He glanced over at Miranda, who mouthed, "Go! Go!"

Hello, Captain Obvious!

Clearly, Lizzie had to take matters into her own hands. "Oh, Ethan," Lizzie said with a nervous laugh, "Gordo could tutor you."

"Yeah, he's really smart," Miranda agreed, smiling. She turned to Gordo, and her frozen smile turned to a glare. Her glance was of the If-You-Don't-Do-This-I'll-Hurt-You variety. Lizzie knew it well.

"And we could help," Lizzie volunteered, smiling up at Ethan. "If you needed it."

"That would be cool," Ethan said. Then he turned to Gordo. "So what do you think, Professor?"

Gordo stared at the test, probably wondering whether it had gotten into a fight with a box of red pens. "Well, I think you could use the help," Gordo said.

"Excellent," Ethan said. He plucked the test out of Gordo's hand and headed down the row of desks. "Catch you later."

Lizzie and Miranda stared after him.

"I wish *my* stereo broke," Miranda said wistfully.

"This tutoring thing rocks, Gordo!" Lizzie said happily, looking over at Miranda. "We have a total in with Ethan." Lizzie and Miranda grinned at each other.

"Guys, relax," Gordo said in a bored voice. "I'm gonna be tutoring a guy who got an eleven on the test."

"That's not so bad," Miranda said.

Gordo looked at her from under heavy eyebrows. "Out of a hundred?" he demanded.

Miranda grimaced and fiddled with one of the slim dark braids that stuck out from beneath her multicolored crocheted cap.

"So—he'll need lots of tutoring," Lizzie said brightly. You'll have your stereo in no time."

Gordo glanced back at Ethan. "With the

amount of tutoring this guy is going to need," he said, "I think I'll be looking at the entire home entertainment system." Gordo sighed. "With surround sound."

Lizzie giggled. She could hardly wait to hang out in front of Gordo's new home entertainment system—with Ethan by her side, of course.

CHAPTER TWO

Matt McGuire and his friend Oscar lay flopped at the base of the couch, surrounded by toys and games. There were drums, trucks, different kinds of battle gear, balls, squirt guns, dinosaurs, skateboards, yo-yos, and every other plastic device known to humanity. Matt was wearing a pirate cap, and Oscar had on a camouflage helmet.

Matt fiddled with a silver claw that was strapped to his right arm. "There's nothing to do," he complained.

Oscar stared at the laser gun in his hand and shrugged. "Nothin'," he agreed.

"Hey, Oscar," Mr. McGuire said as he and Mrs. McGuire walked into the living room. "How're you doing?"

Mrs. McGuire smiled at Oscar.

"He's bored, Dad," Matt said in a tired voice.

Oscar puffed out his cheeks so that he looked like a bullfrog and spat out the word, "Bored."

"There's nothing left to do," Matt griped, gesturing with his toy claw at the mountain of stuff that surrounded them. "We've done it all!"

"You could help out around the house," Mrs. McGuire suggested. "You haven't done that."

Matt looked at his mother from beneath heavy lids. "That's crazy talk, Mom."

"Or help out around the neighborhood," Mr. McGuire suggested. "Old Mrs. Lippin's lawn needs raking."

Matt and Oscar looked at each other and jumped up from the couch. "That's a great idea, Dad!" Matt said enthusiastically.

Mrs. McGuire stared at her husband. It seemed impossible that Matt could be so excited about lawn raking.

"Helping people who can't help themselves!" Matt went on.

"Helping people!" Oscar echoed.

"Mom, we're going to need a couple of costumes," Matt said.

Mrs. McGuire lifted her eyebrows. "Excuse me?"

"Superheroes, Mom," Matt explained. "Me and Oscar are going to be superheroes." He punched his plastic claw into the air.

"Superheroes!" Oscar said in a deep voice.

"Superheroes," Mr. McGuire said eagerly. "I always wanted to be a superhero."

"We're going to patrol the neighborhood and fight crime." Matt did a little superhero fighting move. It was half amazing Ninja warrior, half spazzed-out elementary school kid. Well, maybe more than half spaz.

Oscar winked and pointed at Mr. McGuire with a finger pistol. "Crime," he said, nodding.

"Okay," Mrs. McGuire said patiently. "Does fighting crime include leaf raking?"

Matt cocked an eyebrow. "Are they evil leaves?" he asked.

Mrs. McGuire laughed and looked at her husband. "No."

"Let me know if that changes," Matt said. He turned to his friend. "Let's go, Oscar." The two friends ran out of the room, without even casting a glance back at the horrible mess they were leaving behind.

Mrs. McGuire looked at her husband. For a minute, he looked as though he were going to say something. But instead, he just held out his arm like he was about to fly into the air, and glided off through the room.

Mrs. McGuire shook her head. She could already tell that this was going to be a very long day.

"How hot did Ethan look today?" Lizzie said into the phone later that afternoon. She was sitting on the stairs at home, chatting with her best buds on the three-way.

"Beyond hot," Miranda said from her house.

"You know, I really don't want to be a part of this conversation," Gordo said. Lizzie could hear the gentle thud-thud that told her Gordo was kicking around his Hacky Sack . . . as usual.

"It's okay, Gordo," Miranda volunteered, "we'll stop."

"No, I've got to go, anyway," Gordo told her. "I've got plans."

Lizzie stared at the receiver dubiously. "Plans?" she demanded. "*We* don't have plans. How do *you* have plans?" Gordo hardly ever went anywhere without Lizzie and Miranda.

"I have to go tutor Ethan at the Digital Bean," Gordo explained.

Lizzie and Miranda screamed loudly into the phone together.

"I hate it when you guys do that," Gordo said, clearly annoyed. "Look, I gotta run," he went on. "I'll talk to you guys tomorrow."

Gordo clicked off the phone.

"You know," Lizzie said into the receiver craftily, once Gordo was gone, "I could always use some extra study time."

"Um . . . Digital Bean?" Miranda suggested.

"See you there," Lizzie agreed.

The friends clicked off, and Lizzie ran to find a cool outfit. After all, this was a special occasion—it was the first time in history that she had ever been excited about studying!

Matt and Oscar strode into the kitchen and grabbed a couple of chocolate-chip cookies from the glass jar on the counter.

Mr. and Mrs. McGuire looked at each other.

"See you later, Mom," Matt said. "We're off to fight the forces of evil."

"Dressed like that?" Mrs. McGuire asked, eyeing their outfits. Matt had on a blue sweatshirt with a yellow *M* on the front, red shorts over blue leggings, red galoshes, and a red cape. Oscar was wearing a ragged green-and-yellow-plaid shirt over a green undershirt and ripped jeans. He also seemed to have grown some kind of superhuman unibrow. "Wow," Mrs. McGuire said. "Who are you?"

Matt turned and held up a fist. "Why, I'm Matt-Man," he said in a deep voice. "And this is . . ."

Oscar flexed his muscles. "The Incredible Oscar."

"Don't make him angry," Matt advised his parents. "You wouldn't like him when he's angry."

Oscar growled.

Mr. and Mrs. McGuire cracked up.

"If you need us," Matt went on, "we'll be patrolling the neighborhood. Or in our Fortress of Solitude."

"Be back before dark," Mrs. McGuire told them.

"Have a real good time fighting crime, guys!" Mr. McGuire called.

Matt and Oscar turned to each other.

"Crime!" they shouted, and ran out the door.

Matt and Oscar jogged up the block. They didn't have to go far to find someone in desperate need of help from two superheroes. An old woman was walking down the street, loaded down with two heavy bags of groceries. This was definitely a case for that diminutive duo, M and O.

Matt and Oscar looked at each other and nodded.

"We'll be taking these," Matt said as he and Oscar grabbed the groceries from the white-haired lady and ran off down the street.

"Thief!" the old lady cried, trotting after them. "Thief! Thief!"

"Stop!" Oscar shouted. He and Matt halted in their tracks.

Matt looked down at the curb. "Oh, you're right, Incredible," Matt said. "Superheroes look both ways before crossing the street."

Matt and Oscar looked both ways, then ran across the road.

"Thief! Thief!" the white-haired lady continued to cry out, still huffing after them.

Matt and Oscar finally noticed the old woman and put the groceries down on the ground.

"Thief?" Matt asked. "Where?" He looked around. A man in a business suit, holding a briefcase, was walking toward him. Matt did a few karate moves. The man stared at Matt and kept walking.

Meanwhile, Oscar had spotted another potential suspect—a woman in a tank top and leggings was jogging down the sidewalk. Oscar flexed his muscles, and did a few superhero moves. He finished by scowling at her with his unibrow. The woman just jogged around him.

Huffing and puffing, the old woman finally

caught up to Matt and Oscar. "I'm reporting you to the authorities," she said sternly.

Matt looked at the ground humbly. "No need to thank us, ma'am," he said in a gentle voice.

"We're superheroes," Matt and Oscar explained.

"Just doing our job," Matt went on.

The old lady harrumphed and gathered her groceries, then stalked off.

Just then, a crash and a scream echoed through the neighborhood.

Matt turned to his friend and superside-kick. "We're needed elsewhere, Incredible Oscar. Let's roll!"

Lizzie and Miranda walked into their favorite cybercafé, the Digital Bean, and looked around. Lizzie pointed. Ethan and Gordo were at a table, bent over a pile of books and notebooks. Lizzie and Miranda looked at each other and smiled. Time to start studying! Lizzie thought.

"Hey!" Lizzie said as she slipped into a chair across from Gordo. "What page are we on?"

Miranda pulled up a chair. "Anyone need a pencil?"

The two girls grinned, but Gordo was clearly not amused.

Five seconds later, Lizzie and Miranda found themselves at their own table—across the café from Ethan and Gordo.

"Okay," Miranda said, stifling a groan, "that didn't work. Any more ideas?"

"Yup!" Lizzie motioned for the waitress as she passed by their table with a tray of drinks.

A short while later, the waitress walked over to Gordo and Ethan's table and put two tall glasses down in front of them.

"Um," Gordo said, holding up one of the drinks, "we didn't order these."

The waitress gestured toward Lizzie and Miranda. "They're from the ladies," she explained.

Lizzie and Miranda smiled and waved.

Grinning, Ethan reached for his drink, but Gordo blocked his hand. He sent the drinks back where they came from.

"Hey," Miranda said as she sipped the drink that had been meant for Gordo, "these are pretty good."

"Miranda, we've got to figure out a way to get close to Ethan," Lizzie whispered.

"But he's got, like, a Gordo force field," Miranda pointed out.

"I know," Lizzie said. "I've got an idea— come on." As quickly and quietly as she could, Lizzie scooted their table toward Ethan and Gordo's. Miranda joined in.

Gordo looked up, and Lizzie and Miranda leaned back in their chairs, trying to look casual. When the guys looked back down at their books, Lizzie whispered, "Go."

The two girls started scooting their table again.

Gordo and Ethan looked over at them. Gordo could clearly tell that something was going on, even though Lizzie and Miranda had stopped scooting. That's the problem with Gordo, Lizzie thought—he's so suspicious all the time. Lizzie gave Gordo a little wave. "Hi," she chirped.

The guys bent over their notes again, and Lizzie and Miranda leaned toward their table. "Okay, one last scoot," Lizzie said. She and Miranda scooted their table right up against Gordo and Ethan's. Unfortunately, they scooted a little too hard, and they knocked over their drinks . . . which spilled all over

Ethan's and Gordo's notebooks! The boys jumped away from the table.

"Oops," Lizzie said, staring at the disaster she had caused.

"Hi," Miranda put in casually as the waitress hurried over to clean up the mess. Miranda smiled at Ethan.

"Hey," Lizzie added sheepishly.

"Ethan, why don't we take a break?" Gordo suggested. "We'll attack dividing fractions later."

"But the ladies just got here," Ethan protested.

"Just go get a drink," Gordo snapped.

Ethan gave Gordo a double finger pistol. "Okay, Professor."

Once Ethan was out of earshot, Gordo leaned in toward his friends. "Look," he said, "the only reason you guys are here is because of Ethan. If I was just here studying alone, you wouldn't be here."

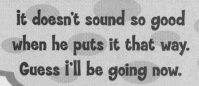

it doesn't sound so good when he puts it that way. Guess i'll be going now.

"Relax, Gordo," Miranda told him. "No need to go nuclear."

"I'm just here so I can earn some money for a new stereo," Gordo said, clearly annoyed. "That's it. So, can you guys, please, just leave me alone?"

"We were just trying to help you, Gordo," Lizzie protested.

Gordo flopped into his chair. "With what?"

"Um, tutoring?" Miranda said.

Gordo laughed. "You must be joking. If I need to go *shopping*, then I'll ask for your help."

What?!

Lizzie glared at Gordo. "Excuse me?" she demanded.

"What are you trying to say?" Miranda's nostrils flared in fury.

Gordo sneered at Lizzie and Miranda. "You guys don't even get As," he said snidely.

Lizzie stood up so fast she nearly knocked her chair over backward. Miranda did the same.

"We get B-pluses, Gordo," Lizzie said, planting her hands on her hips.

"Oh, but I guess we're not smart enough to hang out with you," Miranda added, her voice oozing with sarcasm.

"Good, 'cause I have work to do," Gordo said. He turned back to his books, clearly not affected by Lizzie and Miranda's fury.

Ethan walked up with a drink in his hand. "Ready, Teach?" he asked as he dropped into his chair.

Lizzie and Miranda grabbed their things and stalked off.

Ethan looked after them a moment, then leaned over and put his elbow on Gordo's shoulder. "Looks like you need a tutor on how to deal with the ladies," Ethan said.

CHAPTER THREE

M and O arrived at the scene of the accident—and what they saw wasn't pretty. A girl in a purple helmet had fallen from her matching purple bicycle. It was lying on top of her, and she was clearly trapped beneath it!

The girl looked up at Matt and Oscar and blinked. "Who are you guys?" she asked, eyeing their homemade costumes.

"Remain calm," Matt said slowly. "We're here to help." He surveyed the wreckage, then turned to his friend. "This is a job for the Incredible Oscar," Matt announced.

Oscar flexed his muscles and bent toward the bike. With one superhuman heave, he pulled the bike off the girl and threw it into the street.

The girl jumped up. "Hey!" she shouted. "That's a brand-new bike! I'm telling my dad!"

"No need to tell your dad," Matt said confidently. "Your kind words are thanks enough." He gave the girl a thumbs-up.

The girl glared at him and stomped off toward her bike.

Oscar rubbed his back. "Ow."

Matt patted Oscar on the shoulder. "When performing superhuman acts of strength, always lift with the legs," he advised.

The Incredible Oscar nodded. Maybe for their next adventure, they could find a disaster that wasn't so . . . heavy.

* * *

At lunch the next day, Miranda and Lizzie stared across the patio from where Gordo and Ethan were sitting. Gordo was helping Ethan prepare for the upcoming math quiz, but it didn't really seem to be going all that well.

"Gordo is such a know-it-all," Miranda griped.

Lizzie fiddled with a strand of blond hair. "Yeah, I know," she agreed, "but I still kind of feel bad."

"Why?" Miranda demanded. "He did kind of call us dumb."

"Well, we did kind of use him to get to Ethan," Lizzie pointed out.

"It still doesn't give him the right to be mean," Miranda insisted.

"I guess you're right," Lizzie agreed. She glanced over at Gordo, who was scribbling away in Ethan's notebook. Ethan stared at the paper as though it were the hardest puzzle in the universe while Gordo scribbled on. "We're going to have to talk to him eventually, though," Lizzie said.

Miranda waved her hand. "Fine, so go talk to him."

Lizzie bit her lip and stood up. She should have known that Miranda wouldn't be the one to wave the peace flag. Why did Lizzie always have to do the apologizing herself? She sighed. Oh, well. At least once she said she was sorry, Gordo would say that he was sorry, and everything could go back to the way it was.

Ethan frowned at the math textbook. "Hit me again with what I'm supposed to do?" he said, looking helplessly at Gordo.

Gordo sighed impatiently. "How many times do we have to go over this?" he demanded. "When you're dividing fractions, you have to invert the numerator and the denominator of the second fraction, and then you multiply."

Ethan looked blank.

"That means you flip it over," Gordo said slowly, gesturing with his fingers.

Ethan stared at Gordo's fingers. "Oh," he said. "Okay." He looked down at his notebook, hesitating.

"Hey," Lizzie said as she walked up to them. She leaned against the table and scanned Ethan's notes. "Looks like you guys could use some extra help."

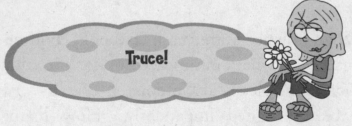

Truce!

"We don't need any help," Gordo said, glaring at Lizzie.

"I need help," Ethan admitted. He looked up at Lizzie with his killer hazel eyes, and she felt as though her heart had melted and turned to liquid goo in her chest. She suddenly loved math.

"Dividing fractions is always really hard," Lizzie said as she sat down next to Ethan. "It's easier for me if I imagine the numbers are something real. Like . . ."—she thought for a moment—"a hair scrunchie." She pulled the scrunchie from her hair and looked at it. One scrunchie isn't really enough to help, she realized. "Who's got a hair scrunchie?" she called.

Everyone on the lunch patio ignored her. Lizzie decided to try again. "Ethan needs hair scrunchies!" she shouted.

Suddenly, Lizzie and Ethan were pelted as every girl on the lunch patio tossed her scrunchie over.

Lizzie decided to use only the ones that had

actually landed on the table. The ones that had fallen in the mud puddle behind Ethan could stay there. "Okay," Lizzie said, arranging the scrunchies on the table, "we have four hair scrunchies."

Ethan stared at the scrunchies, and understanding began to dawn across his face. "Oh," he said, clearly excited, "that's what you call those things!"

Gordo leaned over and pointed at the scrunchies. "Lizzie, we're studying math, not beauty supplies," he said impatiently.

But i come in peace!

She flashed her friend the Look, then

turned back to Ethan. "Okay, what's one half of the hair scrunchies?" Lizzie asked, pulling away two of the scrunchies.

"Two scrunchies," Ethan said.

"Okay, that's one over two," Lizzie explained. She put the two scrunchies back, making four. "Now, what's a quarter of the scrunchies?"

"One scrunchie?" Ethan guessed.

Gordo glanced at Ethan, frowning.

"Good!" Lizzie said. "So that's one over four. Now how many times does one scrunchie go into two scrunchies?"

Ethan thought a moment. "Two," he said, flashing Lizzie a huge grin.

"Excellent!" Lizzie pushed the scrunchies aside and pulled Ethan's notebook toward her. "So, let's look at the problem," she said, pointing at the figures with her pencil. "Now, we have one half divided by one fourth.

Now flip the second fraction and multiply. What do you get?"

Come on, you can get this. i know there are brains under that perfect hair.

"Two!" Ethan said quickly. "That's totally easy!"

"That's what I've been saying for the past half hour," Gordo complained.

"Yeah," Ethan agreed, "but it makes more sense when she lays it down." He gave his chest a double pound and flashed the peace sign at Lizzie.

"Props, Lizzie. Say," he said, grinning at her, "why don't *you* tutor me?"

Lizzie giggled, then looked over at Gordo. Maybe now that he saw that she wanted to help, they could make up and be friends again.

But on second thought, Lizzie guessed that wasn't too likely. Gordo was looking anything but happy.

"I can't believe you said no to Ethan Craft," Miranda said later that day.

Lizzie grabbed her soda and giant chocolate-chip cookie from the counter at the Digital Bean. "I could never do that to Gordo, Miranda," Lizzie said as she and her friend headed to a nearby table with their snacks. "He takes his tutoring really seriously."

"But he's being a total dirk!" Miranda insisted, dropping into a chair. "And he called us stupid!"

"Listen, Miranda, I'm angry about that,

too," Lizzie said. "But I don't want to not be friends with Gordo just because he said something he probably didn't mean."

But for a friend, he's been saying some pretty mean stuff.

"So what are you going to do?" Miranda wanted to know.

Lizzie shrugged. "I'm going to apologize to him for barging in on his tutoring."

"What?" Miranda demanded. "He should apologize to you."

"I know," Lizzie replied, "but friendship is a lot more important than who apologizes to who."

Just then, Gordo shuffled over to their table. "Hi."

"Hey, Gordo," Lizzie said. "Um . . . I wanted to talk to you about something."

"Yeah, I wanted to talk to you, too." Gordo's eyebrows knit together. "I think you guys owe me an apology."

Miranda gaped at him. "What!"

"What!" Lizzie echoed. This was not going according to plan. Of course, Lizzie had been just about to apologize to him, anyway. But now that he had come over and demanded an apology, she totally didn't want to give him one.

Miranda looked up at Gordo and scoffed. "I think you owe *us* an apology."

"For what?" Gordo snapped at her. "You guys are the ones who are using me to get to Ethan Craft. If you want to hang out with him, go ahead. Just don't use me to do it." He scowled at them and stalked off.

Lizzie sighed as she stared after him. She had to admit—he did have a point.

When did my friends become more complicated than my math homework?

CHAPTER FOUR

Matt-Man and the Incredible Oscar sat on the couch in the living room, looking glum. They were listening to a superhuman lecture from Mr. and Mrs. McGuire.

"I don't want to get any more phone calls complaining about you two," Mrs. McGuire said sternly. "So, if you're going to fight crime, you have to keep it to our house."

"And maybe you can use your super-powers to find the TV remote," Mr. McGuire suggested. "I believe it's being held captive by the evil couch monster."

Mrs. McGuire giggled at that.

Matt didn't even crack a smile. "You laugh now, but evil lurks where you least expect it," he warned.

"Evil never sleeps," Oscar agreed, scowling beneath his unibrow.

Mr. McGuire sighed; then he and his wife walked out of the room.

Matt turned to his friend. "You know, there may be crime right in this very house," he suggested.

Oscar's unibrow flew up in surprise. "Really?"

"Yeah!" Matt replied. "All we need to do is create an evil villain, defeat him, and save the family!"

"That's genius!" Oscar cried.

Matt smiled. "They don't call me Matt-

Man for nothing," he said. "Let's roll!" The superheroes leaped off the couch and tore through the house, hot on the trail of their next adventure.

Mr. Dig stood in front of the math class, holding a huge stack of papers. Mr. Dig was a substitute teacher, and he always seemed to be in one of Lizzie's classes. He was a hip young guy, and he had some pretty unusual ideas about teaching. That made him fun—most of the time.

"Mrs. Wortman, your regular teacher, wants you to take this quiz today," Mr. Dig explained, gesturing with the papers. "Me, I don't believe in quizzes. Or tests. Or examinations."

Lizzie let out a whoop, and the whole class burst into applause.

"In fact," Mr. Dig went on, "I don't even believe in grades."

The class cheered louder.

"Learning is a road trip," the substitute said. "It's not the destination—it's the journey!"

Everyone stomped their feet and clapped their hands, whooping wildly.

"Unfortunately, I'm not your regular teacher," Mr. Dig finished. "So take a quiz and pass it down."

The class groaned. But hey, Lizzie thought as she took a test and passed the rest behind her, we should have known that little speech was way too good to be true.

After the quiz, Gordo stood outside the classroom, waiting for Mr. Dig to grade Ethan's test. Lizzie and Miranda were standing there, too. They were pretending to just be hanging out and chatting, but the truth was that they were dying to find out whether Gordo was as good a tutor as he thought he was. And they wanted to get even with him, too. . . .

"So, you say you aced the quiz?" Miranda asked Lizzie in a loud voice.

"Yeah," Lizzie replied, equally loud. "I think I got an A." She emphasized the last word and looked over at Gordo.

Gordo rolled his eyes.

A. A. A.

"Well," Miranda went on, practically shattering the sound barrier with her voice, "maybe next time you can tutor me." She glared over at Gordo.

"Tutoring's hard work, you know," Gordo said to Lizzie and Miranda snidely. "Not everyone can do it."

Ethan walked out of the classroom, holding his test.

"So, how'd you do?" Gordo asked.

Ethan shook his head. "I failed."

Gordo snatched the test from Ethan's hands. "Let me see this." He scowled at the big red F at the top of the paper. "That's impossible!" Gordo insisted. "*I* tutored you!"

Mr. Dig stepped out of the classroom. "Teaching's a tough gig, Mr. Gordon," the substitute said. "I know I make it look easy. But not everyone's cut out to be an educator."

Lizzie smiled at Miranda.

"Listen," Mr. Dig said, turning to Ethan, "I know you've had your nose to the grindstone over this fraction stuff."

Ethan looked confused. "My nose?" he wailed. "I was trying to use my brain!"

Mr. Dig patted Ethan on the shoulder. "It's a good thing you're a handsome boy," the substitute said gently. "Tell you what—since you've been working hard, I'll give you another shot. Tomorrow." He patted Ethan's shoulder and walked back into the class.

"Fine," Gordo said to Ethan. "We'll go over it." He rolled his eyes and sighed. "Again," he added in a bored voice.

Ethan glanced over at Lizzie hesitantly. "I was kind of hoping that Lizzie would help out this time," he said, staring at her with his gorgeous eyes.

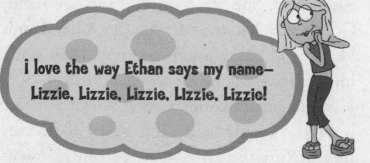

i love the way Ethan says my name— Lizzie, Lizzie, Lizzie, Lizzie, Lizzie!

Gordo looked dubious. "You still want *her* help?" He shrugged. "You know what? Go ahead. Use a second-rate teacher, I don't care."

Lizzie frowned at Gordo. Why was he being such a jerk?

But Ethan didn't seem to notice what a dirk Gordo was being. Or maybe Ethan had just gotten used to it from spending so much time with his tutor lately, Lizzie guessed. "It just made more sense when you laid it down," Ethan said to Lizzie. "So what do you say? Please?" He smiled at her hopefully.

Lizzie glanced from Ethan to Gordo, then back again. She was torn. On the one hand, Gordo was her friend. On the other hand, Gordo was being a jerk and could use some humbling—plus Ethan *was* her crush.

Ethan smiled at her. Gordo scowled at her.

Maybe Gordo will calm down if he sees that he isn't the only smart person in town, she thought. Besides . . . Ethan was still smiling at her. Lizzie giggled nervously.

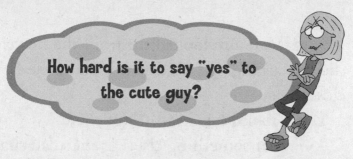

How hard is it to say "yes" to the cute guy?

"Sure, Ethan," Lizzie said finally. "I'll tutor you."

"Cool," Ethan said happily. "This is going to be great."

Gordo stomped off, and Lizzie stared after him unhappily.

"Great," she said, only halfheartedly.

A few hours later, Lizzie walked into the McGuire kitchen. She was wearing a super-cute outfit—black flowered shirt, black pants. There was only one problem. "Mom," Lizzie called, "have you seen my black platforms? They're not in my room, and I can't find them anywhere."

Mrs. McGuire looked up from the flowers she was arranging. "Did you look in the hall closet?"

Lizzie tossed her head. "Not there."

"So, wear something else," Lizzie's dad suggested.

"I'd love to, Dad," Lizzie replied sarcastically, "but all my other shoes are missing." Sure enough, she was standing there, barefoot.

Mrs. McGuire put her hands on her hips. "Lizzie," she said in a warning tone, "is this a trick so I'll take you shoe shopping?"

Lizzie looked at the ceiling and folded her arms across her chest. I can't believe that my own mother doesn't trust me! she thought. Just because I "accidentally" spilled tomato sauce on the world's ugliest dress, then tried to convince her that I needed a new outfit to wear for Flag Day, does she have to treat me like I'm a criminal?

Just then, Matt-Man and the Incredible Oscar leaped into the kitchen.

"It's no trick," Matt said in a deep voice. "It's the work of the Evil Shoe Baron."

Lizzie looked at him doubtfully. "Evil—"

"Shoe—" her mother said.

"Baron?" Mr. McGuire finished.

"Mom," Lizzie said desperately, "I have to meet Ethan at the Digital Bean in twenty minutes and this little"—she gestured to her brother—"Super Zero has stolen all my shoes!"

Matt looked insulted. "Have not."

Lizzie grabbed Matt by the collar. "Maybe you didn't hear me," she said through clenched teeth. "Ethan. Digital Bean. Twenty minutes."

"Okay, Lizzie," Mrs. McGuire warned.

Lizzie let go of her brother's shirt, but she continued to glare at him.

"Matt," Mrs. McGuire commanded, "you

go tell the Evil Shoe Baron that if he doesn't return your sister's shoes in the next ten minutes, he's going to be spending all of his free time in the Fortress of Solitude."

Matt and Oscar gaped at each other, then dashed off.

Lizzie smiled at her mother. "Good work, Mom."

Mrs. McGuire turned back to her flowers. "I've battled the Evil Shoe Baron before."

A minute later, Matt and Oscar returned, hauling a huge black garbage bag. They turned it over, and all of Lizzie's shoes spilled out. A white piece of paper stuck out of one of her platforms.

"A note," Matt said, clearly surprised.

Lizzie gaped at him. Does he really think that he's going to get away with this? she wondered.

Matt pulled the note from the shoe and

read, "'I have given up a life of crime, thanks to Matt-Man and the Incredible Oscar.'"

Lizzie glanced at her father, who smiled. Lizzie sighed. It was incredibly irritating that her parents utterly failed to see how annoying her little brother was. Unless it involved stolen goods or breaking things, Mr. and Mrs. McGuire almost always seemed to find Matt's schemes adorable.

"'If not for their acts of bravery,'" Matt read on, "'I would have taken over the world, one shoe at a time.'" Matt glanced up and held out the note. "It's signed 'the Evil Shoe Baron.'"

"Well, good work, guys," Mr. McGuire said enthusiastically.

Oscar flexed his muscles while Matt grinned triumphantly.

Lizzie scowled at her brother. "Tell any future supervillians that if they touch my stuff, they're history." She grabbed her black platforms and hurried out of the kitchen, grumbling, "I'm outta here."

"Okay," Mrs. McGuire took the note from Matt and glanced at it, "I'm going to ignore the fact that the Evil Shoe Baron's handwriting looks exactly like Matt's, on the condition that your superhero days are over. Inside the house and out. Okay?"

"But," Matt protested, "there's still a lot of evil lurking out there."

"Lurking," Oscar echoed, frowning and gesturing around them.

"And you misspelled 'bravery,'" Mrs. McGuire went on, frowning at Matt.

Matt grabbed the note back from her and peered at it. "I did?"

His mother smiled at him.

It looked like the Evil Shoe Baron's secret identity had finally been revealed. And that meant that M and O were out of work.

CHAPTER FIVE

An hour later, Lizzie was sitting next to Ethan at the Digital Bean. "Okay, let's try dividing fractions one more time," Lizzie said as she leaned over her notebook. She looked down at the table. "We have seven jelly beans."

Gordo peered over at Lizzie and Ethan from his spot on a couch in the corner. Lizzie caught his eye for a moment, and Gordo buried his head in his book.

Ethan looked down at the jelly beans and put one into his mouth.

"No, Ethan," Lizzie wailed. "Don't eat the problem!"

This isn't what i thought alone time with Ethan would be like. But look at that smile!

"Sorry," he said, "I don't get it when it's jelly beans."

Lizzie smiled back. How could she resist such utter hotness when it was smiling her way? "Okay, well, what would you get it with?"

"Uh," Ethan thought for a minute. "Cheerleaders?" he said hopefully.

Lizzie laughed. "Okay. Everybody," she called, "Ethan needs cheerleaders!"

Seven cheerleaders jumped out of their chairs and stampeded over.

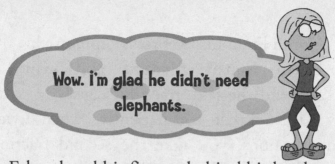

Wow. I'm glad he didn't need elephants.

Ethan laced his fingers behind his head and sat back, grinning.

Lizzie grabbed a whistle from one of the cheerleaders and blew. "Okay," she shouted. "One half divided by one half." She blew the whistle again, and the cheerleaders flew into action. Two of them pulled over short ladders and stood on top of them. Then two cheerleaders came and stood in front of each ladder, so that they formed a clear one over two—or one-half sign. The last cheerleader lay sideways across a stool between the two groups, and held one pom-pom up, and one pom-pom down to form a division sign. One half divided by one half.

Gordo lifted his eyebrows, impressed.

Ethan leaned forward and grinned. "Excellent!" he said, nodding eagerly.

"Okay," Lizzie said patiently, "when dividing fractions, you take the second fraction and flip it upside down. . . ." She blew her whistle again, and the second group of girls started to move. The cheerleader at the top of the ladder climbed down, trading places with the two girls who had been standing in front of it—now they were clearly two over one. "And then you multiply," Lizzie said, blowing on her whistle again. The cheerleader in the middle jumped off of her stool, and held up her arms, planting her feet wide apart to form a giant *X*.

"So that's one times two, over two times one," Lizzie explained, pointing toward the cheerleaders with her whistle. She turned to Ethan. "Which is what?"

"Two over two," Ethan said.

Three of the cheerleaders trotted off. Then two cheerleaders stood on a ladder, and two stood in front of it—two over two.

The cheerleader who had been the multiplication sign trotted back out, then sat back on the stool. She held her pom-poms over her legs, in the shape of an equal sign.

"Which reduces to?" Lizzie prompted. You can get this, she thought, trying to beam thought waves into Ethan's brain.

One cheerleader stepped out of the darkness at the back of the cybercafé.

Ethan grinned and waggled his eyebrows. "Rhonda!" he said, winking at the cheerleader.

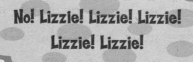

No! Lizzie! Lizzie! Lizzie! Lizzie! Lizzie!

"That's right," Lizzie said with a sigh. "One."

"Lizzie, I really like this math," Ethan said happily.

Lizzie smiled at him weakly, then glanced over at her friend in the corner. Gordo was looking at her. But—for once—the snide look on his face was gone. And Lizzie had absolutely no idea what he was thinking.

"Stay down," Lizzie said to Miranda the next day. They were standing outside the math classroom, trying to peek in to see how Ethan was doing. Mr. Dig was grading the test—but Lizzie couldn't tell whether the marks he was making with his red pen were checks or Xs.

"Why am I so nervous?" Lizzie wailed. "It's not like I'm the one being graded here." But she knew that—in a way—she *was* being graded. Graded on her tutoring. And she knew that with Ethan as a student she could potentially flunk—big time.

"It's okay," Miranda said encouragingly. "He'll pass. He had a great tutor."

Lizzie smiled. She just wished that she felt as confident as Miranda sounded.

"Yeah," Gordo said, walking over to join them, "he did."

Miranda folded her arms across her chest. "You can't be talking to *us*," she said sarcastically. "It's against the brainiac code."

"Look, guys, I'm sorry," Gordo said. He took a deep breath. "I was wrong."

For a moment, Lizzie didn't know what to say. "Oh," Lizzie said, holding her hand to her ear, "can I hear that again?"

Gordo's eyebrows flew up. "I'm sorry," he repeated.

"No, no, no," Miranda corrected, "the second part."

Gordo nodded and looked at the floor. "I was wrong," he said softly. Then he looked up at his friends. "I didn't mean to make anyone feel stupid. If anyone should feel stupid, it should be me," he said sincerely. "I acted like a total jerk."

"Well," Lizzie said gently, "I'm sorry for taking your only student." Lizzie looked over at Miranda. Miranda didn't say anything, so Lizzie gave her best girlfriend a not-so-gentle nudge.

"And for making you feel that we used you to get to Ethan," Miranda added finally.

"Well, I guess none of us got an *A* in friendship," Gordo said.

At that moment, Ethan walked out of the classroom, grinning. "I aced it!" he said happily.

Lizzie took the paper from Ethan's hand. She looked up at him and smiled uncomfortably. "A seventy-two?"

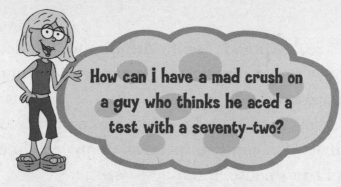

How can i have a mad crush on a guy who thinks he aced a test with a seventy-two?

"You rock, Teach!" Ethan said enthusiastically. He swept Lizzie into a huge hug.

Oh, yeah. That's why.

Ethan took his paper back and grinned at it. He gave it a final glance of triumph and strode off down the hall. Lizzie watched him go. Hey—at least he was happy. And you had to admit . . . a seventy-two was way better than an eleven.

"So," Miranda said, turning to Gordo, "how are you going to get money for your new stereo?"

"I'm not," Gordo said. He pointed to Lizzie. "I'm going to spend all of my free time at Lizzie's house, listening to *her* stereo."

Sponging off my stereo won't cost him a dime! Maybe he *is* the smart one.

"Don't worry, Gordo," Lizzie said as she fell into step with her two best friends. "You can come over any time."

Lizzie McGUiRE

PART
TWO

CHAPTER ONE

Lizzie McGuire and her two best friends, Miranda Sanchez and David "Gordo" Gordon, gaped at the scene in front of them. Lizzie couldn't tear her eyes away—it was like a train wreck, only worse. Larry Tudgeman— the most dooftacular guy at Hillridge Junior high, the guy who put the "eek" in "geek"— was actually trying to act romantic.

Lizzie shuddered.

"Really, Kate?" Larry asked. "You're asking

me out?" His voice was deep and suave—well, deeper and more suave than it usually was, but that's not really saying much. "I knew you'd come around, but tell me, what made you wake up and smell the Tudge?"

Lizzie heaved her bag higher onto her shoulder. What was in Larry's cornflakes this morning? she wondered.

"Was it my charming smile?" Larry went on. "The fact that I've seen *Lord of the Rings* twelve times?"

Gordo choked and shook his head. Miranda just looked stupefied.

"Okay, doll-face—you can pick me up at seven," Larry said smoothly. "Till then, gimme some sugar. . . ." He leaned in for a big smooch.

Lizzie grimaced. "Oh!"

Miranda looked like she was about to gag.

"Was that good for you?" Larry asked.

The mirror inside Tudgeman's locker door,

now marked with his lip prints, didn't respond. I guess it just didn't feel the love, Lizzie thought.

"Okay, so, uh, Tudgeman finally cracked," Lizzie said.

"It's his diet," Miranda said knowingly. "He lives on fish sticks and cream soda."

"He hasn't cracked," Gordo said. "He's just excited about the Sadie Hawkins Day dance. Since the girls ask the guys, this is his big chance." Gordo gave his friends a thumbs-up.

"Okay," Lizzie said, gesturing toward Larry, who was wearing his usual putty-colored shirt with the lime-green collar. "But does he actually think that Kate is going to ask him?" Kate Sanders was queen bee of the school and pretty much the Galactic Empress of Snobbitude. She would never be caught dead within twenty feet of the Tudge—or his putty-colored shirt.

Larry winked knowingly at his locker mirror and gave it the old finger pistol.

"Okay," Gordo finally admitted, "he's cracked."

"You know, Lizzie," Miranda said casually, "no one's asked Ethan to the dance yet."

Yes!

Ethan Craft was the cutest guy at Hillridge Junior High . . . not to mention, the cutest guy in the known universe. He was so hot, he set off fire alarms when he walked by. Lizzie was crushin' on him in a big bad way.

Miranda raised her eyebrows so that they disappeared beneath the straight line of her black bangs. She shoved her hands into the pockets of her low-slung jeans. "You should ask him," Miranda suggested.

Lizzie scoffed. "No." Puh-leeze, she thought. Did Miranda seriously think that she'd suffer through the humiliation of asking out a guy who's so hot he could melt the *sun*?

"Why not?" Gordo demanded. "You're always talking about the guy, but you never, ever do anything about it."

Lizzie sighed and started walking toward her class. She just ignored Gordo. What did he know about being a girl, anyway?

But Gordo wasn't about to give up. He and Miranda fell into step next to Lizzie.

"Lizzie, Ethan obviously likes you," Gordo went on, "and you're gaga for him. So, just ask him, he'll say yes, and we won't have to go over this every single time." He waved his hands impatiently.

Miranda glanced at Lizzie uncertainly, as though she weren't sure how her friend would react to Gordo's irritated hand-flapping. It *was* kind of annoying, Lizzie had to admit. After all, it was easy for Gordo to tell her to do something—there was no way that *he* would get burned. Still, Gordo did have a point . . . how would she ever know if her crush was mutual if she never did anything about it?

"You know what?" Lizzie said, stopping suddenly. "You're right. I don't have to wait for him to ask. I mean, I have my own power," she went on, thrusting her chin forward confidently. "I can see it, and I can be it!"

Suddenly, Lizzie stepped forward, and her foot hooked the wheel of a cart full of library books. She pitched face-forward onto the floor, her arms pinwheeling wildly.

Gordo and Miranda gaped at their friend.

Lizzie glanced up at them sheepishly as she tucked a strand of her long blond hair behind one ear. "Okay," she admitted, looking at the cart, "I didn't see *that*."

* * *

"So, I've been practicing my speech to ask Ethan out," Lizzie said to Gordo later that day. They were sitting together on the lunch patio, and Lizzie fiddled nervously with her glass of juice while she tried to remember the speech she'd spent most of third period writing. She really wanted to practice it before she asked Ethan out, and she knew that Gordo would tell her if she was making an absolute fool of herself. That was one good thing about Gordo—he was pathologically honest. Still, he wasn't as brutal as Miranda could be. Even though Miranda was Lizzie's best friend in the world, Lizzie had to admit that she could be a little harsh sometimes. That was why Lizzie had chosen this moment—while Miranda was off studying in the library—to practice with Gordo.

"You be Ethan, okay?" Lizzie said to Gordo.

"Yo, Liz-zie!" Gordo growled, hitting his best hip-hop pose.

Lizzie sighed. She would have been annoyed with Gordo's imitation of Ethan . . . if it hadn't been so accurate.

"So, Ethan," Lizzie said, tossing her hair nervously, "the Sadie Hawkins dance is coming up soon."

Gordo stared up at the sky and blinked obliviously. "My cousin had a hamster named Joey!" He nodded, like this was the most fascinating piece of news ever.

Wow, Lizzie thought, this is just like having a real conversation with Ethan. Scary. She plowed ahead. "And I was wondering if anyone had asked you yet?"

"Yesterday, I learned how to tie my shoes," Gordo said, nodding again, "but now I forgot."

All right—now the imitation was going too

far. "Okay, Gordo, stop," Lizzie begged. "This is serious." At this rate, it would take her three hours to get through her speech!

"Sorry," Gordo said. "Go ahead."

Lizzie sighed, and tried to remember the end of her speech. "So, Ethan . . . if no one's asked you yet, I was wondering if you might want to go with me." She smiled hopefully.

"Look at the noise I can make—" Gordo said, puffing out his cheeks so that he looked like a gerbil. He slapped his cheeks with the palms of his hands.

How mad can i get? i mean, face it—most of the animals at Dolphin World are smarter than Ethan.

"Gordo," Lizzie snapped, "okay, you were

the one who encouraged me to ask him." She cocked her head and narrowed her eyes at him. "Do *you* have a date yet for the dance?" she asked.

"Eh, I'm not too worried about it yet," Gordo said casually. "I'm at a stage in my life where girls just don't value what I have to offer. I'll have women all over me after I've invented my new software application, bought my own jet, and I'm running, like, five corporations from my island off the coast of Spain. You know, when I'm, like, twenty. Till then, I just have to lay low and get plenty of rest."

Lizzie shook her head, imagining her best friend surrounded by supermodels who would take messages in his office, haul his luggage to his jet, and carry him around his tropical island. Gordo was pretty smart—it *could* happen.

Lizzie's eyes widened as she looked over Gordo's shoulder. A vision of utter tall, sun-kissed, hazel-eyed hottitude strutted confidently onto the lunch patio, greeting people as he passed their tables. It was Ethan, in all of his hunked-out glory.

"Oh my gosh, here he comes!" Lizzie said with a gasp. She looked down at her clothes and did a quick fashion check. Her sheer brown-printed shirt and low-slung jeans were definitely cool, and she was wearing her favorite red crystal choker. Definitely worthy enough to ask Ethan out in. Let's face it, Lizzie thought, he probably won't notice anyway. . . . It's not like he's Sherlock Holmes or something. Which had its pluses and minuses. After all, Sherlock may have been smart, but he always wore that goofy hat and cape—and he was definitely *not* hot.

Lizzie stood up from her seat. It was now or never. She swallowed hard and walked up to

Ethan. "Hey, Ethan—" she said, fiddling with a strand of her hair, "how's it going?" Her heart thudded in her chest, as though it were trying to escape.

"Lizzie, Lizzie, Lizzie," Ethan said as he flashed her his killer smile, "my day is proceeding with fineness."

Lizzie giggled nervously and glanced over at Gordo. "Ask him," Gordo mouthed.

Lizzie took a deep breath. "So," she said, "the Sadie Hawkins dance is coming up, and I was wondering if anyone had asked you yet?" She pulled at the end of her sleeve self-consciously.

Please say no, please say no, please say no!

Ethan gazed off into the distance. "No," he

said, shaking his head. "So far, I'm paddling my kayak alone."

"Oh!" Lizzie glanced over at Gordo again, who nodded encouragingly.

This is it. i'm about to dive into the waters of romance!

Lizzie looked up into Ethan's hazel eyes. "If no one's asked you, I was wondering if you might wanna. . . ." Lizzie shrugged and gave a nervous laugh. Her heart was racing. She could hardly get the words out.

Ethan looked at her expectantly, and she knew there was no turning back now.

"You know," Lizzie said finally, "go with me." She bit her lip and tried to smile.

"Really?" Ethan said. "Me? And you?" He

seemed really surprised. Ethan thought for a moment, then shrugged. "Well, that's really nice and everything, but I always thought of you more as a friend."

Lizzie stared at him. What—what had he just said? This wasn't how the conversation was supposed to end. Lizzie felt like she was floating outside of her body . . . as if this was a scene in a play that she was watching happen to someone else. She touched her hair, just to make sure that her head was still attached to her body, and hadn't floated away, or exploded, or anything.

"I mean, I really like you as a person and everything," Ethan went on, "but I just can't see you as, you know, my romantic type."

Please, stop talking, Lizzie thought. She felt like she had been punched in the gut. She didn't want to hear any more of what Ethan had to say.

"Oh," Lizzie said, blinking back tears. "Okay!" she said, trying to act happy. "That's cool, then. I see you as a friend, too." She wasn't about to let Ethan know that she'd been swooning over him since the Stone Age. "So." Lizzie shrugged as though this moment were no big deal instead of the most humiliating, horrible moment of her life. "We'll be friends."

"Coolness," Ethan said. "So, I'll see you later."

Lizzie felt all of the energy seep out of her body as Ethan strutted away. She just couldn't believe it. Ethan had said no. He didn't like her. After all of that time she'd spent crushin' on him, and thinking about him, and doodling his name in her notebook—he didn't like her at all.

CHAPTER TWO

Meanwhile, in the dark lair of the McGuires' kitchen, Lizzie's little brother, Matt, stood surrounded by beakers and test tubes. He was dressed in a scientist's white lab coat, and had a doctor's reflector on his head. Matt checked his notes and grinned crazily. "Evil Doctor Matt's Sinister Transformation Formula nears completion," he said in a hoarse voice as he lovingly touched the blender on the counter in front of him, which was filled with a mysterious concoction.

"Lanny!" Matt barked. "Bring me the . . ."
—Matt's nostrils flared, and his face looked
sinister—"vanilla extract!"

Matt's best friend, Lanny, who was never
known to speak, held up a strobe light and
shook an aluminum roasting pan to simulate
lightning and thunder. Then he grinned and
limped over to the kitchen counter in an Igor
assistant–type way.

"Hold on there, Lanny—" Matt said quickly.
He walked over to his friend and adjusted the
mini-basketball they had shoved under
Lanny's sweatshirt. "You're losing your hump."

Matt went back to his notes just as Lanny
handed him the dreaded vanilla extract.

Just then, Matt's parents walked into the
kitchen.

"Matt, what are you doing?" Mrs. McGuire
asked, frowning at the blender.

Matt widened his eyes, and an insane look

crossed his face. "Inventing a potion that will usher in thousands of years of evil," he answered with a crazy laugh.

Lanny nodded, grinning eagerly.

"Okay," Mrs. McGuire said slowly, "well, don't break anything." She lifted her eyebrows and walked out of the room.

"And don't touch my pineapple chunks," Mr. McGuire said sternly. "I'm making fruit kabobs later." He followed his wife out the door.

"Now, Lanny—" Matt commanded as he added the vanilla extract to the evil potion, "THROW THE SWITCH!"

Lanny put his gloved hand on top of the blender lid and pressed the ON button. Then, deciding to go with more power, Lanny punched FRAPPÉ. Matt let out another crazy laugh as the blender whirred.

"Enough!" Matt cried, shutting off the blender. He pulled the pitcher from the blender stand and poured the evil potion into two glasses. Matt took a sip.

"Aag!" Matt cried, choking. "Aaa-ha-ha!" he fell to the floor in agony, overcome by his experimental potion, as Lanny watched helplessly.

Suddenly, Matt's choking stopped. "Actually," he said as he hauled himself off the floor, "you know, that's very good." He took another sip of the drink, and Lanny did the same.

Lanny swished the potion around in his mouth, then looked up at the ceiling, deep in thought. Suddenly, the always silent Lanny grinned hugely, his eyes bugging out of his head.

"Don't say another word, Lanny," Matt said. "'Cause, as usual, you're completely correct—" He patted Lanny on the shoulder.

Lanny smiled and waved him off in an "aw shucks" gesture.

"Forget a thousand years of evil," Matt

went on. "We can sell this to our friends and make a fortune."

Matt and Lanny clinked glasses and drank the rest of their concoction. It was evilly delicious.

"Where does Ethan get off, turning you down?" Gordo demanded. It was after school, and the two friends were up in Lizzie's room. Gordo was sitting cross-legged on the bed as Lizzie sat at her vanity table, staring at herself in the mirror and brushing her hair dejectedly. Lizzie had just finished venting about Ethan, and Gordo had been a true friend, giving her all of the standard "he's not good enough for you" lines.

"I don't know," Lizzie said as she swiped at her hair. "I mean, I just always thought he kind of liked me." She shrugged and sighed.

"Well, he *does* like you," Gordo said gently.

"He just, you know, doesn't *like you* like you."

"But why not?" Lizzie wailed. "I mean," she frowned at herself in the mirror. "I'm decent-looking."

"You're very pretty," Gordo said.

"And I'm a nice person," Lizzie went on.

"You're a *great* person," Gordo agreed.

Lizzie squared her shoulders. "And I'm wild and unpredictable."

"You're—a great person," Gordo hedged.

"No." Lizzie frowned at her reflection. "I bet Ethan's looking for some wild, crazy, Drew Barrymore–type of girl." She rolled her eyes. As if. Lizzie couldn't really imagine herself hanging out with the other Charlie's Angels, kicking bad guys in the head. Not exactly my style, Lizzie had to admit.

Gordo thought about Lizzie's theory on Ethan. "No," he said slowly. "Last year he liked Denise Palmer, and she's even duller than you."

Lizzie turned around in her chair and glared at Gordo. Was this supposed to be helping?

"Not to say that you're dull, of course," Gordo said, backpedaling quickly. "Just, you're just . . . not Ethan's type."

"But why can't I be?" Lizzie wailed. "I mean, I can change. I can be anything that he's looking for."

That's right. He wants a party girl, i can be a party girl. He wants artsy, i can be artsy. He wants intellectual . . . oh, who am i kidding? Ethan can't even *spell* intellectual.

Gordo's eyebrows drew together. "But what *is* he looking for?" he asked, holding out his hands. "What do you even know about the guy?"

"Well . . ." Lizzie closed her eyes. "I know that he's a total hottie," she said dreamily.

"Well, there's a rock-solid foundation," Gordo said sarcastically. "We'll go from there."

Lizzie nodded eagerly. Hey, it wasn't much— but it was a start.

The next afternoon, the McGuires' backyard was a total mob scene. Matt had spread the word at school, and by second period, everyone had been dying for a sip of his and Lanny's new Supersonic Tonic. When the last bell rang, the kids stampeded over to Matt's house. Matt noticed that there was even one kid from Lizzie's school—Larry

Tudgeman was standing on line, fidgeting impatiently.

Matt and Lanny had set up a table with a blender and a bunch of cups. "There you go, chief," Matt said as he passed a cup to Roy Patterson. Matt plucked the bills from Roy's hand and stuffed them in his pocket.

"Just sell the stuff, already!" Larry griped from his place halfway down the line. "I've been waiting in line for half an hour—I'm gonna be late for my 4-H Club meeting." All of the elementary school kids stared at Larry. "I raise sheep," he snapped.

"The crowd's getting restless, Lanny," Matt whispered to his friend. Lanny nodded, and Matt knew what to do. As usual, his friend had all of the answers. "Hey!" Matt said brightly as he turned to the crowd. "You know what goes great with a delicious Supersonic Tonic? A few impressions."

The crowd stared at him. "Hoo-ah, there!" Matt cried in a thick southern accent. "Whatcha' doin', throwin' all 'at trash aroun' for? You go pick that up, you little swamp bugs!"

Everyone cracked up . . . everyone except Larry, who stood there, confused.

"That's Mr. Boudreax," Roy Patterson explained, laughing, "the school janitor."

"Lanny," Matt said as he threw his arm around his friend. "I think we're on our way to being the hosts of the hottest spot in town." He smiled as he pictured himself and his best buddy in tuxedos, standing aside as their enormous bouncer let fashionable people past the velvet rope.

"Keep mixing, Lanny," Matt said, nodding at the blender. He turned back to the crowd. "Hoo-ah, I'll go get y'all some pretzels," he called in his thick southern accent. The crowd laughed like crazy. There was no doubt about it—this was going to be great.

"Okay!" Lizzie said as she hauled herself up from behind a tall hedge that bordered the Hillridge Junior High lunch patio. "Do you see Ethan?" she asked, peering over the top of the shrubbery.

"Uh." Gordo adjusted the focus on his binoculars. In a minute, he had Ethan in his sights. "Got him."

"Well, who's he talking to?" Lizzie demanded. She could see Ethan, but without the binoculars she couldn't really tell what he was up to. "What's he doing? What can we tell about him that we don't already know?"

She didn't mean to sound impatient. After all, it was really nice for Gordo to help her with her research on Ethan, especially since Lizzie knew that her guy friend had absolutely no clue why she liked Ethan so much. But still—she wanted the 4-1-1, and she wanted it ASAP!

Ethan was crouching and smiling at something on the ground.

"Well, he's giving some of his sandwich to a pigeon," Gordo said.

"Oh, he likes nature!" Lizzie said, smiling brightly. I knew it, she thought—Ethan has a deep soul. "I can talk to him about that."

"Okay," Gordo said. "Some more pigeons are coming over to get in on it. . . ."

Ethan glanced nervously toward the sky.

"There are lots, lots of pigeons. . . ," Gordo went on.

Lizzie peered up. A flock of pigeons was headed toward the lunch patio. There were so many of them, they nearly blocked out the sun.

"They're kind of swarming him. . . ." Gordo narrated as Ethan leaped over a lunch table. "He's trying to get away . . . he's running. . . ." Ethan did a few karate moves to try to get rid of the pigeons. "They're chasing him!" Gordo said desperately. "Run, Ethan, run!" he cried. Gordo put down his binoculars. "Aw, he just ran into a pole."

"Oh," Lizzie frowned, thinking about what had just happened. "So, he likes nature and he's nearsighted." She tugged on Gordo's sleeve. "Okay, time for some more close-up surveillance."

Gordo stood in the hallway, pretending to flip through a notebook. He was ready to carry out Phase II of Project Date for Lizzie, and everything was in place. Ethan was heading down the stairs. "Hey, Ethan," Gordo said as he fell into step beside the object of Lizzie's crush, "what's up?"

"Hey, Gordon," Ethan said with a wide grin.

"So . . ." Gordo said. "Girls—they're, they're great, right?"

"Aw, yeah!" Ethan nodded at a cheerleader as he and Gordo walked past her. "Girls are awesome."

"Yeah, I'll say," Gordo agreed. "So, you know what kind of girls I like, huh? I like European—you know, real, real sophisticated types."

Ethan nodded. "Like Britney Spears!"

Gordo's eyebrows drew together. He was about to correct Ethan, but decided not to bother. He didn't have enough time to explain something that complicated to Ethan Craft. "Yeah. Sure," Gordo said. "Anyway. So, what kind of girls do you like?"

"I dunno," Ethan said, gazing toward the ceiling. "I always liked kind of mysterious type of women. It's, like, they know something you don't, but you really want to know what that is."

Gordo thought about this. "So, you like girls who know things that you don't. You know," he stopped in his tracks, "that doesn't really narrow it down very much."

"You know," Ethan prompted, "like the type of girls in old detective movies. They're all quiet and dangerous," he said, leaning toward Gordo and waggling his eyebrows, "but you just can't stay away."

"Right," Gordo said, nodding. After all, he was a fan of film noir himself. "I got you."

"You know I never really get to talk about this kind of stuff," Ethan said brightly. "It's kind of nice having someone to talk to about it. Maybe we should hang out more."

Gordo raised his eyebrows in surprise. "Nah, I don't think so," he said. He slapped Ethan on the shoulder. "See ya." Gordo headed around the corner, where Lizzie stood, taking notes.

Mysterious, quiet type, Lizzie scribbled. She

grinned at Gordo. "Come on!" she said, tugging his sleeve. She was excited. This was some good stuff—they were seriously on the case now.

For the rest of the day, Lizzie and Gordo tailed Ethan, getting all of the dirt they could. When Ethan was at his locker, Gordo started up some way-complicated Hacky Sacking. The minute Ethan turned to watch him, Lizzie sneaked toward his locker with her digital camera and took photos of everything he had inside—a close-up picture of a golf club, some Ja Rule CDs, a picture of Pooh and Piglet flying a kite . . . she even took a picture of his pencils. Okay, they're number two, Lizzie thought, as she made a note of it in her notebook. This is great! That's the same kind I use!

Later, while Ethan was sitting on the steps during recess, reading a magazine, Miranda pretended to trip over his foot. When Ethan put the magazine down and turned to help her up, Lizzie grabbed it, and passed it off to Gordo. Gordo flipped it over. *19th Green* was the title—it was all about golf. Gordo shrugged. Lizzie could definitely use this info.

At final recess, Lizzie followed Ethan out to the lunch patio. She whipped out her compact and watched in the mirror as Ethan bought a soda. Lizzie narrowed her eyes, trying to figure out what kind of soda it was. She was too far away to read the label, but she could see the color of the can. Purple. That meant grape soda! Lizzie snapped her compact closed. Perfect.

At last period, Miranda followed Ethan out of English class. She looked both ways, then tiptoed over to where Lizzie and Gordo were waiting by the lockers.

"Okay," Miranda whispered. "So. He loves Roald Dahl books." Lizzie scribbled frantically in her notebook. "Especially *Charlie and the Chocolate Factory*," Miranda went on. She hugged her camouflage notebook to her chest, so that it blended in with the camouflage jacket she was wearing. "He loves the Oompa Loompas."

Oompa Loompas, Lizzie scribbled. She drew a heart around the words, so that she would remember that Ethan was crazy about them. "All right," Lizzie said as she closed her notebook. "I'm ready. Next time Ethan sees me, I'm gonna be the girl of his dreams." She smiled to herself.

A drop of grape soda . . . a teaspoon of golf . . . a pinch of Oompa Loompa, and presto! Okay, the formula needs some work. Maybe a dash more Oompa Loompa . . .

CHAPTER THREE

Matt grinned when he saw who was at the door. "Come on, this way," Matt said with his most charming smile. He was wearing a blue jacket over a printed orange shirt that was open at the neck, and his hair was loaded with even more gel than usual. He strolled through the living room, toward the kitchen. In one smooth motion, he grabbed a plate of nachos from Mr. McGuire's desk and whirled toward the back deck. "Thanks. I need these for the guests."

Mr. McGuire frowned. "Hey!" he called after his son, who had already headed outside. "Those are mine!"

Ignoring his father, Matt swung open the door to reveal a pink neon flamingo . . . and a total party scene. Strings of white lights and Chinese lanterns lit up the backyard, which was crowded with elementary school kids. Matt and Lanny had converted the McGuires' backyard into Club Flamingo—and it truly had become the hippest spot in town for the fifth-grade set. A blond girl in an apron took orders from kids at small tables. Everyone was chatting, enjoying live music, snacking on pretzels, and downing Supersonic Tonic. Lanny was manning the bar while Matt schmoozed the guests.

"Oh, hey, table three wants to hear some P. Diddy," Matt said to the guy at the keyboard. Then Matt wheeled away and walked down the deck stairs with his nachos. He handed them to Larry Tudgeman, who was propped on a stool, drinking his frosty tonic.

"Oh, um, I'm allergic to guacamole," Larry said to Matt.

Matt smiled and slapped Larry on the back. "Tudgeman," he said with a laugh, as though Larry had just told the funniest joke in the world. Then he moved on.

Larry stared after Matt, completely confused.

"Those are mine, you little weasel," Mr. McGuire said as he yanked the nachos out of Larry's hand.

"What did *I* do?" Larry called after Mr. McGuire, who had just stalked off with the plate of nachos.

Matt returned soon after Mr. McGuire had stomped away with the nachos. He led the two guests who had been following him to a small table right in front of the bar. "The best table in the house"—Matt waggled his eyebrows—"for our big spenders."

Miranda and Gordo stared at him in disbelief. *They* were the "big spenders" Matt was talking about. What was going on here?

Gordo cleared his throat. "Thanks, but we're here to see your sister," he explained.

"Yeah," Miranda mouthed.

"Oh, okay," Matt said smoothly, "well, thanks for coming by. Come again soon." He gave a little wave as Miranda and Gordo peered around the backyard, clearly dazzled by Club Flamingo. Finally, they glanced at each other, shrugged, and headed back into the house, where Lizzie was waiting for them.

Matt glared at them as they left. "Deadbeats," he growled. Then he headed back to the bar. He had to take care of his other—paying—customers.

* * *

"So," Lizzie said a minute later, as she walked into the kitchen. "Uh, Ethan said he wanted mystery. Does this hat look like a 'mystery woman' to you?" She adjusted the battered old gray fedora she had stuck over her blond hair and looked hopefully at Ethan and Miranda.

"Are 'mystery woman' and 'bag lady' the same thing?" Gordo asked.

Lizzie shook her head.

Miranda lifted her eyebrows. "Then, no."

Lizzie pulled the hat off her head. Ohhh-kay, that wasn't the response I was looking for, she thought miserably. Then again, at least her friends had told her the truth, and spared her the humiliation of showing up at school in a bag-lady hat.

"On the plus side, I snagged some golf magazines from my dad's waiting room,"

Gordo said. He passed the magazines to Lizzie. "Knock yourself out."

Lizzie flipped through the glossy pages eagerly. Finally, some real Ethan ammo!

Just then, Mrs. McGuire walked into the kitchen, carrying a basketful of clean laundry. She peered over Lizzie's shoulder, and blinked at what she saw. "Honey," Mrs. McGuire said, eyeing the magazines, "are you going to take up golf?"

Lizzie let out a nervous giggle and hugged the magazines against her chest. "Um, yeah, Mom," she said quickly.

"Does this have to do with making Ethan Craft like you?" Mrs. McGuire asked knowingly as she walked over to the counter to fold clothes.

Miranda's jaw dropped, and Gordo's eyebrows flew up, getting lost under his shaggy mop of hobbitlike hair.

"You told her?" Miranda demanded in disbelief, gaping at Lizzie. "Why would you tell her? All parents ever want to do is poke holes in things. You know, poke, poke, poke, poke, poke!" She stabbed the air viciously with her finger. "Poke!"

Here we go. All Mom wants to do is interfere with my life.

"Mom, I really like golf," Lizzie insisted with as much enthusiasm as she could reasonably fake. "It's so fast-paced!"

Gordo shook his head.

"You know, when I was your age," Mrs. McGuire said, not looking up from her laundry, "there was a group of kids that I really wanted to be friends with. And I changed everything about myself to make them like me—I changed the way I dressed, the way I talked, my whole personality. . . ." Mrs. McGuire's voice sounded wistful.

Hey, I guess she doesn't want to interfere. She just wants to tell some pointless story.

"And, in the end," Mrs. McGuire finished, "they still wouldn't hang out with me."

"Wow . . ." Lizzie whispered. "Really?"

Mrs. McGuire closed her eyes and nodded.

Lizzie thought for a moment. "Maybe you didn't do it right," she said quickly, gesturing to her two best friends. "We're going to be upstairs."

Lizzie was glad her mom had told her that story. Now she knew that she'd really have to work hard to get everything just right for Ethan. And she would. She would, if it killed her.

CHAPTER FOUR

"**W**hy, hello, handsome," Lizzie said in a sultry voice as she stepped from the shadows of her math class. She was wearing a slinky black dress and sunglasses, and had on a dark shade of red lipstick. It was her Mystery Woman outfit—and even Miranda had agreed that it looked way glam.

Ethan turned from his locker and stared at Lizzie in surprise. "Whoa. Lizzie, you look . . . whoa." His eyebrows drew together. "Where'd you get those clothes?"

Lizzie looked down at her dress. The truth was, she'd dug it out of a trunk of old clothes that her mom had in the attic. But somehow, that didn't seem like something a mystery woman would say.

Be mysterious, be mysterious. . . .

Speaking in her smooth, Mystery Woman voice, Lizzie answered, "Where do any of us get our clothes, Ethan?"

That was mysterious. i have no idea what that meant.

"I get mine at Dad 'N' Lad Outfitters over on Beacon Street," Ethan said.

"Oh, do you?" Lizzie asked as she sauntered toward Ethan. She pulled off her sunglasses and slowly batted her eyelashes at him.

"Why?" Ethan asked nervously. "Shouldn't I?"

Okay, Lizzie thought, maybe I'm being a little too mysterious. I don't want to confuse the poor guy. . . .

"Lizzie—" Gordo said as he walked up to her, "golf this Saturday, right?" He patted her on the shoulder, as though they made plans for golf all the time.

"Yeah, see you on the first tee," Lizzie called as Gordo made a quick exit.

"You like golf?" Ethan cried. "I love golf!"

Lizzie tossed her hair, as though she were the world's greatest, most confident, most mysterious golfer.

"The problem is," Ethan went on, "I keep hooking my tee shots."

Hmm. Dilemma. She had no idea what a tee shot was. Then again, she thought, it doesn't really matter. Just be vague, she told herself. "Oh, you know what really helps me is . . ." Lizzie pursed her lips, thinking. What information did she know about Ethan that could possibly help right now? "I listen to Ja Rule when I practice," she said quickly, remembering the photos on the inside of Ethan's locker.

"Oh, I love listening to that guy," Ethan gushed. "What's your favorite song?"

Lizzie froze. She had never listened to Ja Rule in her life. "I like golf," she said quickly, flashing Ethan a big smile. "Do you like golf?"

Ethan didn't even notice that she had changed the subject. "I love golf!" he said enthusiastically. "This is so great."

Lizzie smiled flirtatiously at Ethan, and fiddled with her sunglasses. This was working perfectly!

Just then, Gordo reappeared at Lizzie's elbow. "Here's the soda you wanted, Lizzie," he said, handing her a purple can.

"Thank you," Lizzie said in a sultry voice as Gordo hurried off.

"This is scary," Ethan said, staring at the purple can. "Grape soda is, like, my favorite drink ever in the history of the world."

"Oh, is it?" Lizzie asked. She held out the can. "Enjoy." Truthfully, she was glad to get rid of it. She'd hated grape soda ever since second grade, when she'd had three cans after eating a piece of Lucy Wilcox's strawberry birthday cake, and had puked spring colors all over Lucy's rug.

Ethan took the can, staring at it as though it were made of solid gold.

Lizzie slipped the sunglasses back on. "Compliments of Lizzie McGuire."

Ethan stared, dumbfounded, as Lizzie strutted off down the hall in her slinky black dress, touching her hair. This was going so perfectly!

Ethan looked down at his grape soda and popped it open. Soda fizzed from the can, squirting in every direction. "Aggh, my eyes!" he shouted.

Hearing the shout, Lizzie cringed, but kept walking. Okay, so the plan hadn't gone *perfectly*. But—she had to admit—it was pretty close!

"Drink up, sunshine," Matt said as he passed a glass of Supersonic Tonic to a redheaded girl from his class who was visiting Club Flamingo. "It'll make a man out of you."

The girl looked at the drink suspiciously, then took the cup and walked off.

Larry Tudgeman appeared on the back deck. "How ya doing, Matty?" he called.

"TUDGE!" Everyone in the bar said, lifting their glasses as Larry strode down the steps.

"Heya, Tudge," Matt said, "how's life treating you?"

Larry pulled a stool up to the bar. "Like a baby treats a diaper," he said. "So set me up." He held out his hand, and Matt pressed a tonic into it.

Just then, a thick-necked kid strode through the McGuires' kitchen and into Club Flamingo. He looked around at the crowded backyard and scowled. "All right," he boomed, "what's the deal here?"

"Uh-oh, Lanny," Matt whispered to his friend. "It's Sonny Mazerowski." Sonny was the biggest bully in their school—literally. He was so enormous that when he sat down in the back of the bus, all of the other kids had to rush to the front, just to make sure that they didn't pop a wheelie.

"Hey," Sonny said as he turned to Roy Patterson, "I don't see you around my house anymore."

Roy blinked nervously at Sonny through his round eyeglasses.

"How's that supposed to make me feel?" Sonny demanded.

"I'm sorry, Sonny," Roy said quickly. "I'll be there tomorrow."

Sonny narrowed his eyes and pointed at Roy. "More like right now," he said threateningly.

"Okay. Sorry." Roy put down his drink and scurried away.

Larry put his drink on the counter and turned to Matt. "What happens at that guy's house?" Larry asked.

"Sonny's parents have a seventy-inch TV and a satellite dish," Matt explained. "He charges people to watch in the afternoons."

"A satellite dish?" Larry said, lifting his eyebrows. Matt had just said the magic words. "Patterson," Larry called, "wait up!" He hurried after Roy, who had already disappeared into the McGuires' kitchen.

Sonny stormed over to the bar and knocked over the stool that Larry had just left empty. "You're costing me money," he barked at Matt. "All of my customers are hanging out here."

Matt shrugged. "Yeah, so?"

Lanny continued to wipe a glass calmly. He didn't even look up at Sonny.

"So, I'm shutting you down," Sonny growled. "And I want your drink recipe."

Lanny lifted his eyebrows at Matt.

"Oh, yeah?" Matt said, his voice dripping

with sarcasm. "Well, I want a solid-gold Indy car. Doesn't mean it's going to happen."

Lanny grinned and shook his head at Sonny.

The bully reached over the bar and grabbed Matt by the collar. Matt let out a little squeak as Sonny dragged him halfway over the countertop. "Let me break it down so you'll understand," Sonny snarled in a low voice. "You can shut down, or you can start spending every lunch period at school in the trash can"—he narrowed his eyes into dangerous slits and glowered at Matt—"outside the cafeteria."

It took less than one millisecond for Matt to weigh his options. "Okay, everybody out!" he shouted. Sonny released Matt's collar as Lanny hurried the customers out of the club. Lanny flicked his bar towel at the kids as they scurried out of the backyard.

"Everybody out!" Matt repeated. "Out! Get out of here! Shoo! Gogogogogo!"

Club Flamingo was empty in no time.

"Okay," Sonny said, nodding to the pitcher of Supersonic Tonic. "What's in this?"

"Well, some strawberries," Matt said as Sonny began to scribble the recipe down on a napkin. "Ice . . ." Suddenly, Matt had an idea. Sonny had big muscles . . . but his brain was pretty tiny. Maybe there was still a way to get even with him, after all.

"Three cloves of garlic . . ." Matt went on, "half a cup of pickle juice . . . a jalapeño pepper . . . two cups of fish oil . . ." Sonny kept scribbling.

Matt grinned as he pictured Sonny whipping up a nice, tall glass of this new-and-improved drink recipe. For his sake, Sonny better have a supersonic stomach.

* * *

"I just can't believe that you like chili-pastrami-tortilla-dogs, too," Ethan said as he and Lizzie carried their trays across the lunch patio.

"Oh, yeah," Lizzie lied, staring down at the disgusting mess on her plate, "they're my favorite." She plopped her tray down on the table and slid into the seat next to Ethan. "Yum, yum, yum."

'Cause who really needs unclogged arteries, anyway?

Lizzie was wearing a yellow shirt and a baby-blue golf vest, topped off with a blue-and-yellow tropical-print visor. It was an outfit that screamed, "See you on the green!" At least, that was what Lizzie hoped it screamed.

Because it was definitely screaming something.

"You know what would go perfect with this?" Lizzie asked as Ethan took a huge bite of his lunch. "An Everlasting Gobstopper."

Ethan nearly choked on his chili-pastrami-tortilla-dog. He chewed quickly, trying to down the enormous bite he had taken. "Hey, that's from *Charlie and the Chocolate Factory*," he said, pointing at Lizzie. His mouth was still half full. "That's, like, my favorite book."

Lizzie smiled as she popped a potato chip into her mouth. Once again, her plan was moving along nicely. How could Ethan resist a woman he had so much in common with?

"You know, it's incredible," Ethan went on. "We both like the same things."

"It *is* incredible," Lizzie agreed. Of course, it's also not true, she thought. But that wasn't really important right now. The important thing was, the plan was *working*. It was definitely time to take things to the next level. "So," Lizzie said slowly, "are you, uh, going to the Sadie Hawkins dance with anyone tonight?" Lizzie looked at Ethan hopefully.

"Nope," Ethan replied. "Still flying solo."

"Um." Lizzie did her best to make her voice sound casual. "Well, we should go together. . . ."

"Oh, uh . . ." Ethan looked uncomfortable. "I thought . . . I thought we had already understood each other about that. About how we're just going to be friends."

"Oh." Lizzie looked away, confused. "Well, uh . . ." she said uncertainly. "We just have so much in common."

"I know," Ethan admitted. He looked down at his tray, thinking. "It's weird. It's, like, if I wrote everything we both like on paper, we'd be perfect for each other." Ethan glanced up at Lizzie. "And I like you and all, but there's just no . . . oh, shoot—" Ethan frowned. "What's that subject in high school that I'm never going to pass?"

Lizzie suspected that there were a lot of high school classes that Ethan might not pass, but she kind of had a clue which one he was talking about. "Chemistry?" Lizzie guessed miserably.

"Yeah," Ethan said. "There's just no chemistry." He looked at Lizzie. "Does that make sense?" he asked gently.

"No," Lizzie replied. "But I guess this stuff doesn't always make sense."

And the great thing about that is, i'm still a kid, so i only have to deal with this stuff for another, like, eighty years.

"I'm sorry," Ethan said. He really sounded like he meant it. Not that it made it any easier. If anything, Lizzie thought, having Ethan be a nice guy just makes it harder.

"Yeah," Lizzie told him. "Me, too."

CHAPTER FIVE

Lizzie stood in the kitchen, staring blankly into the refrigerator. She'd been standing there for ten minutes, but she wasn't seeing the usual assortment of leftovers, condiments, and soda cans. No—all Lizzie could see was Ethan's face when he had told her that he didn't want to go to the Sadie Hawkins Day dance with her . . . again. She couldn't stop thinking about it. Ethan's words kept echoing in her mind: *There's just no chemistry. No chemistry. No chemistry.* Over and over again. She just didn't get it—how could she feel something so strongly when Ethan felt nothing at all? It didn't seem possible. Lizzie was thinking so hard that she didn't even hear her parents walk into the kitchen behind her.

"Maybe there's something better on another channel," Mr. McGuire joked gently.

Lizzie jumped. "What?" she asked. "Oh. Sorry." Lizzie closed the fridge and walked over to the counter, sighing heavily. A box stuffed with golf clubs, Gobstoppers, Ja Rule CDs, and grape soda sat on a stool next to her. Lizzie guessed she wouldn't be needing those things anymore.

"You okay, sweetie?" Mrs. McGuire asked.

"Uh . . . yeah . . ." Lizzie lied. She tossed the ugly yellow-and-blue visor and a golf magazine into the box.

"Giving up golf, huh?" Lizzie's mom asked.

There's the silver lining. Golf pants look terrible on me.

"Well, I like the old, nongolfing Lizzie better," Mrs. McGuire said softly.

Lizzie looked at her mom closely. She was really being cool—but it wasn't helping all that much.

Yeah? Why didn't you say so? Why didn't you tell me that changing myself to please Ethan was never gonna work? Wait—my diary says you did. Oh, well, never mind.

"We're sorry the whole thing didn't work out for you," Lizzie's dad said.

"If there's anything at all that we can do, you just let us know," Mrs. McGuire added.

Huh. They don't want to control my life. They just want me to be happy.

Lizzie managed to smile weakly at her parents. "Thanks," she said. She didn't really feel like talking, though, so she headed out toward the deck.

Mrs. McGuire started after her daughter, but Mr. McGuire put a gentle hand on his wife's shoulder. "There's really nothing more we can say to her," he said. "She'll bounce back from this."

Mrs. McGuire sighed. "You're probably

right." She looked up at her husband. "And since when did you become such an expert on teenage girls?"

"Well, I got dumped by enough of them," Mr. McGuire replied with a laugh. "I got cut loose by every girl I ever liked."

Mrs. McGuire lifted her eyebrows at her husband.

"Until I met the perfect woman," he added quickly.

Mrs. McGuire nodded. She had to admit—her husband had made a nice save.

Lizzie walked up to the bar at the now-empty Club Flamingo and slid onto a stool. Matt was wiping down the countertop with a white towel. Lanny was packing up the chairs, and getting ready to shut off the twinkly white lights and Chinese lanterns for the last time.

"So, uh, you got any more of that

Supersonic Tonic left?" Lizzie asked Matt awkwardly.

Matt flipped a cup into the air and caught it expertly before pouring Lizzie a drink. "Ethan trouble?" he guessed.

Lizzie took a sip of tonic but didn't reply.

"You know," Matt went on, "if you drink this every time a guy dumps you, I'd better make a million gallons."

Lizzie looked at her brother. She knew he was just kidding—that it was one of his usual smart-aleck lines—but it hurt, anyway.

"Uh—" Matt said uncomfortably, "this is the part where you call me a squeaky runt, or a spiky-haired weasel, or something."

Lizzie just sighed.

Matt looked down at the bar and fiddled with a stack of cups. "Sorry."

"He didn't want to go out with me," Lizzie said quietly.

"You know, Ethan's a cool guy and all. . . ." Matt told her. "He's just kind of . . ." Matt crossed his eyes and let his jaw hang slack. "Duhhh."

"Yeah," Lizzie agreed. "But knowing someone's wrong for you doesn't change the way you feel."

Matt nodded.

Lizzie finished her drink and pushed herself away from the bar. "How much do I owe you?" she asked.

"It's on the house—" Matt said. He wiped the counter with his towel. "I'm out of business. Sonny Mazerowski shut me down."

Lizzie sighed again. "Life's unfair."

"You said it, sister," Matt agreed, nodding. "You said it."

Just then, Miranda and Gordo walked onto the back deck. Miranda was wearing a pink Indian-print dress with lace at the neck, and

Gordo was actually wearing a blazer. They were clearly ready for the Sadie Hawkins Day dance.

"Hey," Miranda said to Lizzie as she joined her friend at the bar. "How're you doing?"

"Oh, not bad," Lizzie told her. "My parents kept pulling the 'any guy would be lucky to go out with you' thing, so . . ." So clearly that cured everything, Lizzie thought dismally—*not*.

"You want to go to the dance, anyway?" Gordo asked.

"Nah," Lizzie shoved a strand of hair out of her face and looked away. "I don't have a date."

"Neither do I," Miranda said. "Well, I thought of someone I would ask," she admitted, "but it turns out Brad Pitt's married."

Lizzie laughed weakly.

"And, as predicted, poor old Gordo got

zero invites." Gordo held up his fingers in a big circle. "The big goose egg. Good morning, good afternoon, and good night." He shook his head and sighed.

Lizzie looked at her friend. Gordo actually looked pretty bummed about not getting a date. She guessed they had both struck out. "So, uh, dance with me," Lizzie suggested.

Gordo lifted his eyebrows at Lizzie.

"Play it, Lanny," Lizzie called.

Lanny tossed aside his bar rag. He pulled a stool to the keyboard and began to play a slow tune.

"Come on," Lizzie said, grabbing Gordo's hand and dragging him to the middle of the backyard. "Let's go." Gordo stumbled after her, obviously embarrassed. Still, he let Lizzie put her hands on his shoulders. He put his hands on her waist, and they began to dance to the music.

Miranda reached behind the bar and grabbed Matt's hand. "It's Sadie Hawkins Day," she announced as she pulled him next to where Lizzie and Gordo were dancing. "I am not going to be the wallflower." She smiled over at her friends, who grinned back.

"For the record," Gordo said to Lizzie, "you're much better at being Lizzie than at being Ethan's type."

Lizzie thought about that. "Yeah, well, it was fun for a while," she admitted, "but I think I would have gotten sick of not being me." And I would have literally gotten sick if I'd had to drink that grape soda, she added mentally.

See, if i were still "Ethan's type," i would have no idea how to tie my shoelaces.

"Well, I like you better as you," Gordo went on. "Although that Mystery Woman thing was kind of"—he waggled his eyebrows— "rrrrowwwwrrr."

Lizzie smiled. I wonder what Mystery Woman would have to say to that? she thought. Something that made no sense, no doubt. "Oh, you think so?" Lizzie asked mysteriously.

Gordo looked confused. "Isn't that what I just said?"

"Did you?" Lizzie asked in her Mystery Woman voice. "Did you really?" Lizzie and Gordo cracked up, as the friends danced the night away at Club Flamingo . . . for the last time ever.

STRAPPED FOR CA$H

STRAPPED FOR CA$H

Adapted by Jasmine Jones
Based on the series created by Terri Minsky
Part One is based on a teleplay written
by Melissa Gould.
Part Two is based on a teleplay written
by Nina G. Bargiel & Jeremy J. Bargiel.

EGMONT

PART
ONE

CHAPTER ONE

Lizzie McGuire had it all worked out. She'd practiced in the mirror that morning, with her friends during lunch, and even after school. When she got home, she was happy to find her parents right where she wanted them— in the kitchen, making dinner. Her mom stood over a bubbling stew, and her dad was on salad duty, with knife and red pepper in hand.

"Hey, honey, how was school today?" Mrs. McGuire asked.

Lizzie cautiously approached her parents and put on her best "I'm your perfect daughter" smile. "Oh, school was wonderful. Did you guys have a good day?"

"It was okay," said Mr. McGuire.

"Yeah, it was just fine." Mrs. McGuire glanced at Lizzie, suspiciously.

"Oh, look." Lizzie beamed at her parents. "You're making your famous stroganoff. Oh, it's my favorite!"

"Are you in trouble, or do you want something?" Mrs. McGuire asked flatly.

"Oh, um . . ." Not expecting her parents to read her so well, Lizzie was kind of thrown off guard.

i knew the stroganoff was going too far. Last time, i tried to feed it to the dog. And we don't even have a dog.

"Well, you know, Mom, Dad. I'm . . . I'm getting older now, and I have a lot more needs. And I don't want to bug you guys every single time that I need to buy something, so, um, um . . ." Lizzie took a deep breath. Now or never, she told herself. It was time for the clincher. "I want a raise on my allowance."

How can you argue with that?

"No," Lizzie's parents said at the exact same time.

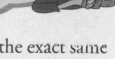

I guess that's how.

Okay, time to change tactics, Lizzie thought.

"But all of my friends got raises!" she argued.

> Give 'em the sad eyes. They can't say "no" to the sad eyes.

Lizzie blinked and looked at her parents with her trademark pleading puppy-dog eyes.

But Mrs. McGuire wasn't falling for it. "Oh, enough with the sad eyes," she said.

"Listen, if there's something you really need, just ask us," Mr. McGuire explained, in the logical, matter-of-fact tone that drove Lizzie crazy. "We'll get it for you."

"You know, that's just it, Dad! I don't want to have to ask anymore," Lizzie said. "I'm not a little kid. I need freedom."

"Well," said Mrs. McGuire, "when you

start earning money of your own, then you can be free with that. But until then, you have to manage with your allowance the way that it is."

"Fine," Lizzie huffed, unable to imagine the conversation having gone any worse. She stormed off, feeling depressed with a capital *D*.

Yeah, well, your stroganoff tastes like an old shoe! An old, smelly, burnt shoe!

That night, Lizzie met her two best friends, Gordo and Miranda, at their favorite cyber-café, the Digital Bean. "And they said no about raising my allowance. Just like . . . just like *that*. Like, 'no,'" Lizzie complained.

"Well, did they say why?" Miranda asked,

as the three friends sat down at a table in the back of the Bean.

"I think it's because they want complete and total control over my life," Lizzie said. "Forever."

"Not forever," Gordo pointed out. "Just until you turn eighteen. You've only got a couple more years to go."

A couple more years? Don't i get time off for good behavior?

Lizzie felt rotten. "I just hate running to them for every little thing."

As Miranda nodded her head in agreement, she noticed a sign by the cash register. It read BUSBOY WANTED. "Lizzie, you could get a job," she said.

Lizzie went on talking as if she hadn't even heard Miranda. "When I'm at the mall and I want a pair of jeans, I want to buy them."

Miranda pointed to the sign and raised her voice. "Lizzie, you could get a job."

"I need independence and freedom," Lizzie went on. "But no, they won't let me have that."

When Gordo glanced up, he noticed the sign, too. "Lizzie, you could get a job," he said.

"A job?" Lizzie looked at Gordo like he was some sort of genius, which wasn't exactly a stretch. He was sort of one of the smartest kids in school. "What a great idea. I could get a job."

It was only when Miranda slumped over and dropped her head onto her arms that Lizzie noticed her. "Oh, I'm sorry. Were you saying something, Miranda?" Lizzie asked.

Miranda banged her head against her arms a few times before answering. "Huh? Oh, no.

I think getting a job is a great idea." Looking up, she pointed to the busboy sign yet again. "I think they're looking for a new busboy."

i can clear plates. i do that at home for free!

"I could be the new busboy!" said Lizzie, as she smoothed down her hair. "How do I look?"

"You look like a busboy," said Gordo, encouragingly.

"Okay," Lizzie said. She was a little bit nervous. She'd never had a job before—not a real one that didn't involve washing cars for world peace or manning the "Save the Rain Forest" bake sale cash register, anyway. Still, the blue sign said help was wanted here, and Lizzie wanted to help.

"Go get 'em," said Miranda.

Lizzie glanced at her friends hopefully and then headed to the counter.

She returned a few minutes later with a huge grin and the BUSBOY WANTED sign. "Looks like there's a new busboy in town!" Lizzie said.

McGuire's batting a thousand on the job front.

"So when do you start?" Gordo asked.

"I start tomorrow," Lizzie answered. This was way too cool.

"But I thought we were all supposed to hang at the mall tomorrow," Miranda said.

"Oh, well, we can hang here instead. It'll be fun," Lizzie replied.

"Are you sure?" Gordo asked. "We don't want to get you in trouble."

"Oh, no," Lizzie said. "I think it'll be fine. Plus, I think I can swing some free drinks for my friends."

Gordo's eyes widened. "Free?" he asked. "Free is my favorite number."

Back at the house, Matt and his friend Reggie were playing catch in the backyard. Well, Reggie was playing, anyway. Matt just stood there, staring off into space. When Reggie lobbed the football, it sailed right past Matt, who didn't even blink.

"Oh! Matt, is something up with you?" Reggie jogged past Matt to retrieve the football, which had landed in the bushes. "You didn't even notice I threw the ball."

"Oh," said Matt sadly.

"Dude, I know something's wrong. Even Lanny said you've been awful quiet lately." That really said something. Their friend

Lanny was quieter than a mime. When he walked, you couldn't even hear his footsteps.

Matt slumped down in a wicker chair. He hadn't been this depressed since he'd faked being sick and his mom had forced him to eat three bowls of beet soup. Sighing, he decided to come clean to his friend. "It's just . . . Reggie, I don't think Melina wants to be friends with me anymore."

"I thought things were good," Reggie said, more than a little confused. "She hasn't gotten you into trouble for days."

"Exactly," Matt said. "And Jared Ferguson has been in detention for nearly a week now. It doesn't take a genius to put two and two together." Matt rested his chin against his knuckles and slumped his shoulders. "Melina's moved on."

"You're better off without her, man," Reggie said.

Matt knew Reggie was trying to make him feel better, but it wasn't working. Yes, Melina was ignoring him, but Matt's problems were bigger than that. "It's just, I don't understand girls."

"Nobody understands girls," Reggie said. "Except, maybe, a girl." Suddenly, a huge smile broke out on Reggie's face.

Matt knew his buddy was on to something. "Talk to me," he said.

"Maybe you need to talk to a girl," Reggie suggested.

"But I don't know any," Matt argued.

"What about Lizzie?" asked Reggie.

"Ewww!" Matt made a face. "Lizzie's not a girl. She's my sister."

"But she's the closest thing you've got," Reggie reminded Matt.

Matt rested his chin on both knuckles. "So, *this* is what rock bottom looks like."

CHAPTER TWO

The next morning, Lizzie wolfed down her breakfast and picked up her plate right away.

Mrs. McGuire yelled out, "Hey, Matt! Hurry up, honey, or you're gonna be late for school!" Then, turning to Lizzie, she said, "Sweetheart, leave all that."

"Oh! It's no problem, Mom," Lizzie answered brightly, thinking she could use the practice. She picked up her dad's plate of bacon and eggs, not noticing he was still in the process of eating.

Mr. McGuire held his fork in midair, and stared hungrily at the plate in Lizzie's hand. "That's okay, I was nearly done, anyway," he said.

Mrs. McGuire blinked at Lizzie, curiously. "Okay," she said. "You've been good for two days in a row. What have you done?"

Lizzie was so excited, she could hardly stand still. "Um, okay. I got a job!"

"A job?" asked Mr. and Mrs. McGuire at the same time. They were so good at responding in synch, Lizzie wondered if they practiced their reactions beforehand.

"Yeah," Lizzie said, proudly. "I am the new busboy at the Digital Bean."

Mrs. McGuire looked at Lizzie, concerned. "Well, honey. I think you should've talked to us before getting a job."

"But now I don't have to ask you guys for money." Turning to her dad, she said, "And now you don't have to raise my allowance. It's a win-win situation."

"But, Lizzie," Mr. McGuire said, still eyeing his half-finished breakfast that hovered in front of him in Lizzie's hand. "Work is a huge responsibility." He lunged his fork at his eggs, but they were out of reach.

"Yeah, you have your homework and your friends and your chores. I mean, it's a lot to handle," said Mrs. McGuire.

"But, Mom," Lizzie said. "It's just a busboy job. I mean, I'll clean some tables, I'll see Gordo and Miranda, and I'll do my homework in between."

Mr. and Mrs. McGuire exchanged glances. It was another thing they were great at—talking to each other without actually exchanging words. Lizzie just waited.

After what seemed like ages, Mrs. McGuire turned to Lizzie and said, "I still think it's a lot to take on . . . but you know what, you're old enough to make your own decisions, so—"

"Thanks, Mom! Thanks, Dad," said Lizzie. "I can totally handle this."

"Welcome to the rat race," Mr. McGuire said, as he took back his eggs.

Lizzie headed off to school, so excited she was practically bouncing.

As she left, Matt walked into the kitchen. "Mom, Mom, where's Lizzie?" he asked, in a panicky voice.

"She just left," Mr. McGuire said.

"Oh, I really needed to talk to her," Matt said, very disappointed.

Mrs. McGuire said, "Oh, well, you can talk to me, sweetie."

"Sorry, Mom," said Matt. "But I need to talk to a girl."

As Matt left the kitchen, Mr. McGuire chuckled quietly.

CHAPTER THREE

Lizzie's first shift at the Digital Bean was going great. After she served a customer a muffin, she straightened her blue apron, and then sat down at the counter. I just served my first muffin, she thought. This is so cool!

This job thing rocks! i'm free! i'm independent! No one tells me what to do!

Just then, Lizzie's manager, a tough-talking

woman who was about ten years older than she, walked up and placed a purple paper napkin and a fork and knife on the counter. "Lizzie, front and center! I need you to roll silverware."

No problem, Lizzie thought, as she swiftly rolled the silverware and handed it back to her manager. Ha! If I had known working would be so easy, she thought, I would have gotten a job years ago!

Lizzie imagined all the cool things at the mall she'd be able to buy now. New jeans were just the beginning. There were jewel-encrusted hair clips and some dangly earrings, not to mention that cute zebra-striped tank top. Maybe she'd even get something nice for her mom.

"Impressive," the manager said, interrupting Lizzie's brief daydream. "Now you can turn pro." Lizzie's boss pointed to an enormous heap of silverware that was piled at the end of the counter.

With no choice, Lizzie got to work. Fifty minutes later, her fingers were stiff from silverware rolling, and she thought to herself that if she had to touch another fork, she'd run for the door, screaming in terror.

When her manager approached again, Lizzie asked, "Oh, what now?" in a weary voice.

"You're done for the day," the manager told her.

"Really?" Lizzie asked hopefully.

"No," the manager said. "But that gets them every time. Now, you're going to take all the rolled silverware and put it on the floor."

"Great." Lizzie tried to remember why she had been so excited about being a busboy. But nothing was coming to her.

As she lifted the tray full of rolled silverware, she realized that it was way too heavy. It was also a bit unbalanced. Suddenly, the tray tipped over, and all of the silverware went tumbling to the floor.

"Lizzie, just a hint," the manager said. "When I said, 'put it on the floor,' I didn't really mean 'on the floor.'"

"Yeah," said Lizzie. "I got it."

"Good," said the manager. "And I'm gonna need you to roll some more silverware."

Lizzie rested her head in her hands and moaned.

Half an hour later, Matt showed up at the Digital Bean. He sat down on a stool and said to the waitress at the end of the bar, "Juice. No ice. And keep 'em coming."

"Excuse me, worm," said Lizzie. "I don't pick up after you at home, and I don't plan on picking up after you here! Okay? So, don't make a mess."

As his third juice slid down the counter,

Matt grabbed it and downed it in one gulp. "Lizzie, I can't believe I've sunk this low, but I really need to talk to you."

Lizzie suddenly became serious. Even though Matt was an annoying worm, he *was* still her brother. "Matt, what's it about?"

"You see, it's about Melina. She's, uh . . ."

Before Matt could spit out the tragic news, Lizzie's boss showed up. "Uh, Lizzie? What are you doing?"

Lizzie looked at her, wondering why she was asking such an obvious question. "I'm talking to my little brother," she said. "Can I get a second?"

"What do *you* think?" the manager asked.

Whoops, thought Lizzie. "I think that I'm not being paid to talk to my brother," she covered.

"You're psychic," the manager said, pointing over her shoulder toward a dark corner of the café. "So, you already know the ketchup bottles need to be refilled."

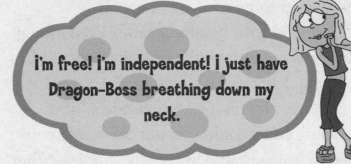

I'm free! I'm independent! I just have Dragon-Boss breathing down my neck.

"Okay." Lizzie walked off toward a table that was filled with a whole army of ketchup bottles—and they were ready to attack!

As she got to work, Miranda and Gordo entered the café.

"Hey, Matt," Gordo said.

"Uh, where's Lizzie?" Miranda asked.

"Over there." Matt, motioned toward the land of the empty ketchup bottles.

"How's her first day?" Gordo asked.

They watched as Lizzie inspected and then

shook a ketchup bottle. It didn't seem to be empty, so she stared into the opening and squeezed it a little. This turned out to be a huge mistake, because as she did so, a huge glop of ketchup landed on her face.

"Pretty much like that," said Matt. "Juice me," he said to the waitress. Seconds later, she slid another glass to Matt, who caught it expertly.

Miranda glanced at the many empty glasses on the counter. "Uh, you're hitting the juice pretty hard there, aren't you, Matt?"

Matt said, "You wouldn't understand. You see, I need to talk to a girl, but Lizzie's the only one I know, and she's busy."

"Matt? I'm a girl," said Miranda.

Matt looked at Miranda, and it was like he was seeing her for the very first time. She wasn't just Lizzie's friend. She was Lizzie's friend with soft brown eyes, and a cute, pink, furry thing in her hair. Suddenly, his day seemed brighter. "Hey, you are, aren't you?" he said.

"Nothin' gets past you, does it?" Gordo asked.

Matt ignored him and turned his attention to Miranda. "You see, it's about Melina. She's getting someone else into trouble. Someone who's not me."

"And?" asked Miranda, not really seeing the problem.

Matt downed another glass of juice, slammed his hand against the counter, and blurted out, "Juice me."

He turned back to Miranda. "I think she's moved on," he explained.

Lizzie's little bro was already into girls? Miranda looked at Gordo, not knowing what to say.

Gordo stifled a laugh. "I'm gonna let you handle this one," he said.

Miranda turned back to Matt. "You know, Melina doesn't realize how good she has it."

"What do you mean?" Matt asked.

"Matt, you're a great kid," Miranda replied. This was news to Matt. "I am?" he asked. Miranda nodded. "Totally."

"You really think so?" Matt asked again, not really believing what he was hearing.

"Absolutely," said Miranda. "And if Melina can't see that, then she's not worth it."

Matt stared at Miranda, who was looking less and less like his sister's best pal and more and more like a supermodel.

"Not bad," Gordo whispered to Miranda, genuinely impressed with her advice.

"Wow," Matt said. Suddenly his heart felt lighter and kind of fluttery. "You really think I'm a great kid?"

"Yeah, I really do." Miranda answered, sincerely. "And there are plenty of other girls out there who'd be lucky to go out with you."

"Wow, thanks." Matt suddenly realized, after all this time, that Miranda wasn't just pretty—she was totally hot!

"Sure, no problem." Miranda shrugged.

Just then, Lizzie yelped loud enough for the entire café to hear.

"Maybe we should catch up with Lizzie later. . . ." Gordo said, motioning toward Lizzie who looked like she'd been attacked by a ketchup-spitting monster. Her once-clean apron was now red and sticky. She had ketchup in her hair, ketchup on her face, and ketchup underneath her fingernails.

Gordo, Miranda, and Matt cringed at the sight. ". . . when she's not so tomato-y," Gordo added.

"You could come over after dinner." Matt suggested eagerly, assuming his sister would be ketchup-free by then.

"Cool," said Miranda, totally oblivious to Matt's drooling over her. "Tell Lizzie we'll see her then."

As Gordo and Miranda left the Digital Bean, Matt looked after Miranda with puppy-dog eyes. "It's a date," he said with a sigh.

CHAPTER FOUR

Later that day, Gordo, Lizzie, and Miranda walked through the McGuires' backyard. Little did they know that someone was watching them from inside.

"So how was your first day in the working world?" Miranda asked.

"Besides sticky," Gordo added.

"Totally busy," said Lizzie. "I didn't stop working the whole time I was there."

Lizzie's job was way different than she'd thought it'd be. She figured she'd be clearing the occasional table and filling a water glass here and there, while getting paid to chill with her friends. But back in the real world, Lizzie's day was insane. If she wasn't rolling silverware, she was mopping the floor. If she wasn't mopping the floor, she was clearing plates. And if she wasn't clearing plates, she was filling bottles of sticky, old ketchup.

Her feet ached, and her hands were all prune-y and wrinkled from washing dishes. She just wanted to earn some cash to buy some clothes, and maybe the new scent she tried at the mall, but the only perfume she was wearing now was eau de ketchup!

Gordo noticed someone peeking out from inside the house, but when he looked back, the blinds closed. Thinking it must have been Lizzie's mom or dad, he turned his attention back to Lizzie's comment. "Isn't that the definition of a job?" he asked.

"Uh, yeah, but I didn't think it would be so much . . ." Lizzie paused as she tried to come up with the perfect word.

"Work?" Gordo asked. He looked up again, and this time he was sure someone was spying on them. He saw Lizzie's brother peeking over the half-door from inside the house, but then a second later, Matt was gone. Gordo shook his head.

Meanwhile, Lizzie and Miranda continued their conversation, completely oblivious to the fact that someone was watching them. "Yeah, but when payday comes around, you'll be swimming in cash," Miranda said, thinking, first Matt, now Lizzie—I give great advice!

"Exactly," said Lizzie, her spirits brightening a little.

Just then Matt rose up from behind a lawn chair, startling everyone so much that they screamed out in unison.

"Lizzie, Mom wants you in the kitchen," Matt said.

"Don't ever do that again, Matt!" Lizzie yelled. Turning to Gordo and Miranda, she softened her tone. "I'll be right back." To Matt she warned, "And don't bug my friends."

As Lizzie walked away, Matt handed Miranda a card. "Here," he said before darting off.

"Thanks," Miranda said, totally confused.

Gordo smiled. "I think Matt's over Melina."

"I know," Miranda nodded. "I give such good advice."

"No, no, you're missing my point, Miranda. He's over Melina because he's got a crush on you."

"Puh-lease," Miranda said, looking at Gordo like he was crazy. "This is *Matt*. He's just giving me a *thank-you* card."

"Yeah," said Gordo, knowing what was coming next.

Miranda opened the card. Inside was a picture of a couple holding hands—cute, except for one problem. That couple was Matt and Miranda! Matt had glued pictures of the two of them over the original couple's faces!

Miranda heard scary movie music playing in her head as it dawned on her that Lizzie's little brother *did* have a crush on her. A big, bad one, in fact. "Ahhhhhh!" she screamed in terror.

"I hate being right all the time," said Gordo, who was clearly enjoying this new turn of events. "So, when you and Matt get married, are you gonna move in here, or are you gonna get an apartment, or what?"

As she closed the card, Miranda just shuddered, trying to shake off her acute case of ickiness.

Gordo walked into the house, but Miranda opened the card again and gaped. There was her face, still glued right there next to Matt's. She was truly stunned by this horror of horrors. And looking at it was just as bad the second time around.

The Digital Bean was hopping the next afternoon, but Lizzie was too busy to enjoy it. She ran around, bussing tables, cleaning up messes, and rolling more silverware. Her shift had started just a couple of hours ago but she was already exhausted and counting the minutes till she could leave. Gordo was right. She'd had no idea an after-school job could be so much, er . . . work!

Miranda and Gordo walked in and scanned the place for an empty table. Gordo broke out his Hacky Sack and started kicking.

Lizzie marched over to them. "Hey, I'm off

in fifteen minutes, so just sit over there and don't order anything!"

She grabbed Gordo's Hacky Sack. "And Gordo, will you please stop this. Okay? You're gonna knock something over, and I'm gonna have to clean it up."

As Gordo and Miranda sat down, Miranda said, "Guess we can't talk to the new, working Lizzie."

"Probably not. But you've got the next-best thing," Gordo said, pointing to Matt, who had just rolled in on his scooter. "Your boyfriend."

"He is *not* my boyfriend," Miranda replied through gritted teeth.

Gordo looked at Matt's new license plate, which read MATT ❤ MRNDA.

"But he hearts you, Miranda!" Gordo joked.

As Miranda sat down, Matt scooted over.

Just when she thought it couldn't get any worse, she noticed he was sporting a large button with a picture of her face on it!

"Fancy meeting you here," Matt said. Then he glared at Gordo and said in a voice dripping with jealousy, "Gordo."

But Gordo didn't mind at all. He was having too much fun. "Hey, I like your button, man."

"Thanks," said Matt. "I made it myself."

This was way too much for Miranda—she was freaking out.

Matt, trying to be an attentive "boyfriend," asked, "Something wrong, sunshine?"

Sunshine? Miranda could barely speak. "I . . . I just need a drink."

"One drink, two straws. Comin' right up," said Matt as he sped off.

Miranda scowled at Gordo. "You could be a little more helpful, Gordo."

Gordo shrugged with pretend innocence. "What? I said I liked his button."

When Miranda narrowed her eyes at him, he said, "I'm sorry. It's just so . . . funny."

Gordo wasn't the only one enjoying his afternoon at the Digital Bean. Kate Sanders, the head cheerleader, and Claire Miller, the junior captain (aka Lizzie's two least favorite people), sat watching Lizzie like hawks. They were totally pleased with the fact that she was scrambling around like a cheerleader without her pom-poms. Deciding that Lizzie wasn't quite stressed enough, Kate knocked over Claire's strawberry smoothie. Pink goop oozed onto the table and dripped onto the floor. Lizzie spotted the mess and stomped over.

"Okay, which one of you did this?" she asked, angrily.

"It's called an accident, Lizzie," Kate said as she shot Lizzie a nasty look.

Around Kate and Claire, there is no such thing as an accident.

"Sure, it was an accident," Lizzie said sarcastically.

Just then, her manager walked over. "It'd be really nice if there was a busboy around to clean this up," she said. Glaring at Lizzie, she added, "Hey, look who's here."

"But they did it on purpose," Lizzie argued.

Kate looked up at the manager and blinked innocently. "Honestly, it was an accident."

"Lizzie," the manager said. "Get a rag.

Clean this up. And apologize to these customers."

Life was so unfair! Lizzie wanted to argue.
"But, but . . ."

Apologize to Kate and
Claire? i don't think so.

"Or I could put the BUSBOY WANTED sign
back up," the manager replied.

i'm free. i'm independent.
And . . . And . . .

Lizzie looked from the manager to Kate
and Claire. She wanted to throw up! "Sorry,"
she mumbled.

i don't know which is grosser—having to apologize to Kate and Claire, or cleaning melted smoothie off the floor.

Lizzie got a rag and started wiping up the mess, clearly grossed out.

"Oh, look," Claire cooed. "You missed a spot." Claire and Kate high-fived each other and flipped their hair over their shoulders.

And a few minutes later, Lizzie's shift was finally over.

CHAPTER FIVE

The alarm clock blared next to Lizzie's bed, but she felt like the buzzing was going off right between her ears. She couldn't believe it was Saturday morning already.

She'd been having the worst nightmare: She was a busboy at the Digital Bean, and she was covered in ketchup, and she had to clean up after Kate and Claire . . . oh, wait. . . . As Lizzie woke up, she realized that the nightmare was actually just her life!

She picked up her alarm clock and smothered

it with a pillow. Then she buried her head underneath another pillow.

Suddenly, she heard a knock on her door.

"Come in," Lizzie called.

Her dad walked into the room. It was Saturday and he was in jeans and a baseball cap, looking relaxed. Unlike Lizzie, who was wearing a too-tired-to-do-anything look on her face. "Hey, honey. Don't you have to work today?" her dad asked.

Lizzie answered sadly. "Yes."

"Let me rephrase this," Mr. McGuire said, gently. "Are you planning on going to work today?"

"I don't really have a choice," Lizzie mumbled from under her pillow.

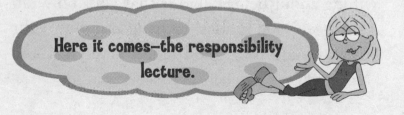

Here it comes—the responsibility lecture.

"Of course you have a choice," said Mr. McGuire. "You could always quit."

Lizzie sat up. Was she hearing him right?

Who are you and what have you done with my real dad?

"Dad, I'm not gonna quit. Earning my own money makes me happy," Lizzie said.

"You don't look happy," Mr. McGuire observed, all too accurately.

"Well, that's why it's called a job," Lizzie reasoned. "Because it requires a little bit of work."

"Lizzie," her father answered. "The great thing about being a kid is that your only job is to get good grades, to hang out with your friends, and be a good kid. You've got those covered."

"Well, Dad, this is what I really want to be doing. I mean, I hate running to you guys for every little thing. I want to be independent."

"Okay. But independent is harder than it looks," Mr. McGuire said. "Listen—I'm your dad. You're supposed to ask me for stuff."

"Well, then can I ask you for a ride to work because I'm gonna be really late," Lizzie said.

"Okay," Mr. McGuire answered.

"Okay," Lizzie whispered, getting up.

"Yeah, she's going," Mr. McGuire called down to his wife.

Hearing that, Lizzie collapsed back into her bed for her last few seconds of rest for the day.

That afternoon, Miranda looked around her room, which was filled wall-to-wall with balloons—heart-shaped red ones, pink ones, orange ones, white ones, and yellow ones.

Some had pictures of Matt's face printed on them and some had pictures of Miranda's.

She pushed through the helium and rubber jungle, found her phone, and dialed frantically. "Gordo! Good! You're home. Okay, Matt's crush on me has gone totally loco," Miranda said, punching the psycho balloons out of the way.

"Ah," Gordo said, totally enjoying the moment. "Isn't that great?"

"No!" Miranda said. "It's horrible."

"Maybe for you," Gordo replied. "But for me, it's endlessly entertaining."

Before she could respond to her so-not-funny friend, Miranda had another call. "Ugh. Hang on, that's my other line."

Feeling completely stressed, Miranda clicked over and shouted, "Hello!" into the phone.

"I love the way you say hello," said a lovesick Matt, on the other end.

"Oh, Matt." Miranda's heart sank. "Hey, can you hang on a sec?"

"Till the end of time," Matt swooned.

Miranda clicked back over to Gordo. "It's Matt! What do I say?"

"I dunno—he's *your* boyfriend," Gordo said. "Talk about what you usually talk about."

"Not helping, Gordo," Miranda said between clenched teeth.

"So, uh, why don't you tell him you just want to be friends?" Gordo suggested, not adding that girls used that line on him all the time.

"Friends? I can do that." Miranda clicked back. "Matt," she said, as she pushed another balloon out of the way. "I'm so glad you called."

Matt took a deep breath and crossed his fingers. "Hey, I was wondering maybe if you wanted to go bike-riding later."

"Like, on a date?" Miranda asked. It was such a sweet gesture. She hated to shoot the kid down.

"Um, yes?" asked Matt.

"Uh, can you hang on?" Miranda clicked back to Gordo.

Meanwhile, Matt crossed his fingers and arms and toes and legs, in hopes that Miranda would say yes.

She pushed a balloon away from her head, exclaiming, "He just asked me out on a date!"

"So I guess the 'let's-just-be-friends' thing didn't work?" Gordo asked.

"Oh, Gordo, what do I say?"

Gordo shrugged. For once, he had no idea what to do. "Well, if you don't do something quick, you're gonna be Mrs. Matt McGuire."

Miranda rolled her eyes and clicked back to Lizzie's little brother. "Hey," she said.

"So will you go?" Matt asked, squinting his

eyes shut and crossing his arms and fingers again.

"Well . . . I . . . I mean . . ." Try as she might, Miranda just couldn't come up with a decent excuse. "Sure."

Matt dropped the phone and started doing a victory dance. "Yes! Yes! Yes!"

After Miranda hung up, she popped balloons left and right.

CHAPTER SIX

Back at the Digital Bean, Lizzie's day wasn't getting any better. The café was packed, and to make matters worse, Kate and Claire had front-row seats! Every time Lizzie walked by, they pointed and whispered, rolled their eyes, or just snickered.

A stuffy man in a tie banged his spoon on the table and motioned for Lizzie. "Could you get me another spoon, please?"

Lizzie looked down at the bagel on his plate, confused. "Why?" she asked.

"Because this spoon is dirty," the man said.

"Sir, you're eating a bagel," Lizzie pointed out. "You don't need a spoon to eat a bagel."

"I need a clean spoon," the man said, raising his voice as if Lizzie were hard of hearing.

"Okay, sir. I'll be right back," said Lizzie, tiredly.

As she walked toward the counter she noticed something fly through the air. A young kid was giggling as he smashed up a muffin and then threw the crumbs all over the *clean* floor. The *very* clean floor. The *very* clean floor Lizzie had *just* cleaned! Frustrated, but trying to keep her cool, she bent down and picked the crumbs up.

"Isn't he a cute kid?" the muffin boy's dad said with a smile.

Lizzie just shook her head. She grabbed a

spoon from the bin of clean silverware, went back to the lunatic bagel guy, and placed it on the table. "There you go, sir. There's your clean spoon."

"You just touched that spoon after cleaning the floor," said the man. "That spoon is dirty. I need a clean one."

Ignoring Kate and Claire's giggles, Lizzie went back to the counter to wash her hands. But before she got a chance to, her boss said, "Lizzie, the garbage won't take itself out."

"I'll be there in a second, okay?" Lizzie responded.

"Okay." The manager waited for literally one second and then said, "Now."

Now i know why no one else applied for this job.

The garbage was an overflowing mess. Lizzie crammed things down from the top.

Meanwhile, muffin boy continued to throw crumbs on the ground, and even worse, his dad was now doing the same thing. The spoon guy tapped his knife against the side of his plate and motioned Lizzie over again. Grabbing a clean spoon, she brought it to him. "There you go."

The spoon guy was horrified. "You just touched the garbage and didn't wash your hands! That spoon is dirty. I need a clean one."

Lizzie didn't have the patience to argue with him, so she walked to the sink, washed her hands, grabbed a spoon, and headed toward the table.

Seeing her approach, Claire spilled her raspberry smoothie onto the floor. Lizzie didn't notice and slipped, landing flat on her back. *Oof!*

"Oops," said Kate. "Sorry." Her voice could not have sounded any less apologetic.

"Accidents happen," Claire said, in an equally nasty tone.

Fuming mad and in a lot of pain, Lizzie got up off the ground. "You know what? No!"

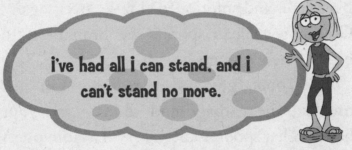

i've had all i can stand, and i can't stand no more.

"Okay, listen up, that was not an accident. All right? And my job is hard enough without you two brats making it worse."

Hearing the commotion, the manager walked over. "Lizzie," she started.

But Lizzie interrupted. "And you see this mess? I'm not cleaning it up. I'm not cleaning up after anybody in this whole room!" She pointed to the muffin boy. "And you, little muffin boy! You see this right here? You eat this muffin or you put it in the trash can. But keep it off my clean floor." She walked over to the spoon guy. "And Mr. Spoon Boy? You don't need a spoon to eat a bagel." Lizzie grabbed the bagel and started waving it in front of his face. Then she shoved it into his mouth before he could say a word in protest. "I came here trying to do my job so I didn't have to ask my parents for money anymore. I want to be free, and I want to be independent! But no! Obviously, that's not gonna happen."

"Uh, Lizzie," said the manager.

"And you!" Lizzie spun around and pointed at her boss. "You're always telling me what to do, and always asking me for things! And that's not being free or independent at all! Now is it?"

"You're absolutely right," said the manager. "You done?"

"Yes," said Lizzie. "Yes, I feel a lot better now."

"I am so glad," said the manager with a small grin. "You're fired."

"Fired?" asked Lizzie. "I'm fired?"

"Eh, don't feel too bad," the manager said. "I go through three busboys a month."

When Kate and Claire burst into a fit of nasty giggles, Lizzie just glared.

But then she realized: no more sticky ketchup bottles, no more cleaning up after Claire and Kate, no more muffin boys, and no more rolling silverware. Maybe being fired wasn't so bad, after all. . . .

CHAPTER SEVEN

Gordo and Miranda walked through the McGuires' backyard. "Just like we practiced," Gordo coached.

Miranda repeated. "Matt, you're a really great kid but I think we should just be friends."

Gordo shook his head, sadly. "I can't believe you're gonna break Matt's heart."

Miranda shot him a glare. "You know what? You just want me to keep this going for your own sick amusement."

"Well, yeah," Gordo said. He'd thought that was obvious.

"Wait," said Miranda.

They walked inside to find Matt on the couch, playing a video game. Hearing them enter, he looked up. "Miranda, you're early. I thought we were going bike-riding later. I mean, I haven't even had time to wrap your present."

"Yeah, well, we need to talk," said Miranda.

"Is something wrong?" Matt asked.

"Well, kind of." Miranda squirmed, thinking this was so much harder than she'd thought it would be. She glanced at Gordo, remembering the speech they'd practiced. Opening her mouth, she found that the words wouldn't come out.

Misinterpreting the look, Matt narrowed his eyes at Gordo. "Is it someone else?" he asked.

Gordo said, "Uh, no. Don't worry. She's all yours."

"Gordo!" said Miranda, wondering whose side he was on. Turning to Matt she said, "Matt, no—there's no one else."

Matt grinned. "Phew! That's good 'cause I don't think I can return these." He held up a couple of T-shirts. Both pictured supersized Matt heads, and one had an arrow that read, I'M WITH . . .

Miranda gasped. "What do I say to that?" she whispered to Gordo.

"I say you go out with him." Gordo laughed. "Those shirts are pretty cool."

Miranda shot Gordo her "you're not helping at all" look. She realized she'd have to handle this on her own.

Just then, Melina entered the room. Looking back and forth between Miranda and Matt, she said, "So, the rumor is true?"

"Hello, Melina," Matt said, nervously.

"Listen," said Melina, shooting Miranda an icy glare. "Just because you can't find a guy your own age doesn't mean you can steal mine."

Miranda was so confused. What was going on?

"You're just a rebound girl!" Melina continued. "So keep your distance. 'Cause if anybody's gonna get Matt in trouble, it's gonna be me. Got it?"

Matt looked from Melina to Miranda, and then back to Melina again. "You really do like me!" Matt said.

"Let's go," Melina said.

Matt jumped off the couch as if it were on fire. "Sorry things didn't work out," he said to Miranda.

"Now!" shouted Melina.

"Coming, my angel," Matt sang.

He grabbed the shirts and followed Melina outside. "Look, I made these for you. . . ."

Miranda and Gordo were left standing in the McGuire living room, totally stunned. "Well, that was easy," Miranda said.

Gordo looked at her. "You do realize that you just got dumped by Matt."

Miranda gave him the evil eye. "We're not talking about this ever again. Especially to Lizzie."

"All right"—Gordo folded his arms over his chest and grinned—"rebound girl."

"That was talking about it," Miranda warned, through clenched teeth.

As they walked out, they ran into Lizzie.

"Hey, you guys," she said. "What are you doing here?"

"You know, it's a funny story," Gordo said, following Lizzie into the kitchen.

Miranda slapped the back of his head, and Gordo closed his mouth.

"So, how was your day?" Miranda asked.

"It was great." Lizzie coughed. "Until I got fired."

"Oh . . . well, what happened?" Miranda asked.

"You were caught drinking straight from the shake machine, weren't you?" Gordo said. When Lizzie and Miranda both shot him a crazy look, he shrugged his shoulders. "What? That's what I would've done."

"No," Lizzie explained. "I wasn't as polite as I should've been to the customers."

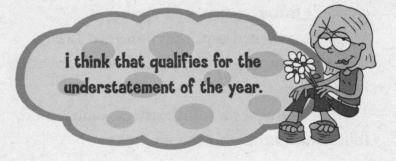

i think that qualifies for the understatement of the year.

"It wasn't pretty," Lizzie went on.

"So I take it the money train has stopped rolling," Gordo said.

"Gordo," Lizzie said. "I don't think that the money train ever took off from the station. Besides, if I'm always working, how am I gonna have time to spend the money?"

"Good point," Miranda said.

Lizzie looked at her friends. "So, what's up with you guys? I feel like I haven't seen you in days. What's been going on?" She walked to the fridge and opened it up.

Gordo was about to give Lizzie the 4-1-1 on the "Miranda-Matt-Melina love triangle" when Miranda shot him another warning look. "Nothing," he said. "Nothing at all."

"You guys hungry?" Lizzie asked as she peered into the fridge.

"Keep it zipped," Miranda said to Gordo under her breath.

Meanwhile Lizzie spotted a pink, heart-shaped cake in the fridge. She took it out and placed it on the counter. "Ooh, cake," she said, distractedly. She peered back inside for something to drink. "Milk?"

Miranda stared down at the cake, horrified. It read, "I ♥ Miranda." Gordo started to laugh, silently.

"Yeah," Miranda said. Since Lizzie's back was still turned, Miranda wiped the frosting off the top of the cake with her fingertips, smearing off her name and the rest of the message. Not knowing what else to do with the evidence, Miranda shoved it into her mouth.

Lizzie turned back around and stared at her friend, whose face was covered in pink frosting.

"Frosting's the best part," Miranda mumbled with her mouth full, grinning bashfully. Talk about eating your own words!

Lizzie looked at her friend's messy face. She wondered if some frosting had fallen on the floor or messed up the counter. She almost got ready to grab a rag to clean it up, but decided against it. Her days as a busboy were behind her for the time being. And she couldn't have been happier!

PART
TWO

CHAPTER ONE

After school on Thursday, Lizzie broke out her new candle-making kit and got started. Pale yellow wax bubbled on a double burner on the stove, and her can-shaped molds lined the counter. She smelled her two latest candles. One was purple, and one was red. Mmm . . . vanilla-scented bliss! Next she measured out wax for some blue and pink ones.

Mrs. McGuire was preparing dinner nearby, but took a break to peer over Lizzie's shoulder. "Honey, don't let that cloth get too close to that burner."

"I know, Mother." Lizzie glared at her mom, thinking, there's nothing worse than a backseat candle-maker. Still, she picked up the dishcloth and tossed it away from the stove.

Mrs. McGuire went back to pounding on a large slab of meat. "I'm sorry, I'm sorry. I know you're not a small child," she said to Lizzie.

The phone rang, and Mrs. McGuire answered it. "Hello? Oh, hey, Debby."

Lizzie dropped a new wick in the mushy wax as she listened to her mother's end of the conversation.

"Well if you can't baby-sit tomorrow night, you can't baby-sit." Mrs. McGuire smiled as she held the phone. "No, I'm not angry at you for calling me last minute. Okay, bye-bye," she said, sweetly. Hanging up, she went back to the meat. But this time she really pounded on it!

Lizzie raised her eyebrows but otherwise

ignored her mom's obvious attack on the poor cutlet.

A few moments later, Mr. McGuire and Matt came home from Matt's soccer practice. Matt, who was almost at eye level with the night's dinner, asked, "Why is Mom mad at the meat?"

"Oh, hi, honey," Mrs. McGuire said, easing up on her full-force thrashing. "How was practice?"

"Zachary Greenwald accidentally fell on a sprinkler head and had to get stitches," Matt said, sadly.

As Mrs. McGuire shuddered, Matt slowly smiled and said, "It was really cool."

"And Matt came very close to actually kicking the ball, didn't you, champ?" Mr. McGuire asked.

"Oh, yeah." Matt puffed out his chest proudly.

Mr. McGuire stood over him and mouthed silently, "No way!"

"Oh, Debby Gottschalk called," said Mrs. McGuire. "She can't baby-sit tomorrow night."

"Well, is there anyone else we can get?" Mr. McGuire asked. He'd been looking forward to a night out on the town all week and was clearly disappointed.

"Oh, oh," Lizzie chimed in. "Don't get that Olivia Skibbens. She makes us listen to country-western, nonstop." Lizzie shuddered as she had a nightmarish flashback to the time when she and Matt were forced to line dance in the living room, for two hours straight! She was so brainwashed by the twangy tunes that the next day at the mall she actually checked out a pair of cowboy boots!

Matt had a different fear. Making a face he said, "Not Mrs. Harvey. She smells dead."

"Well, we're not going for Tammy up the street, either," said Mrs. McGuire, as she remembered handing over stacks of cash at the end of a night, unhappily. "'Cause she makes more an hour than I do."

"No way we're going with Mrs. Jaffe," said Mr. McGuire. "Who lets a boy drink an entire quart of maple syrup?"

Matt grinned as he recalled that night. With his mind buzzing from the best sugar rush ever, he'd raced around the kitchen island, feeling like the winning car in the Indy 500! "I liked her," he said.

"Well, we've gotta find somebody," said Mrs. McGuire.

Suddenly, a perfect idea popped into Lizzie's head. She looked at her parents, hopefully, wondering how best to approach the topic. "Um, well, I was thinking . . . I was thinking maybe I could—"

But before she managed to say the words, her parents finished her sentence for her. "Baby-sit?" they asked at the exact same time, both sounding equally horrified.

Wow! They must have *both* read the "How to Be an Overprotective Parent" newsletter this month!

Mrs. McGuire said, "Honey, we've talked about this, you know, we just think you're . . ." Her voice trailed off as she gently tried to come up with the right words.

"You're too young," Mr. McGuire said, firmly. "No."

"When will I be old enough to trust? When I'm fifty?" Lizzie exclaimed.

"Maybe," Mr. McGuire answered. "We'll see." He walked over to the stove to check out dinner. "Where's Mrs. Doubtfire when you need her?" he wondered as he dipped his finger into the pot and took a taste.

Wrinkling his nose, he turned to Lizzie and asked, "This isn't cheese, is it?"

"It's candle wax," said Lizzie.

Matt cracked up, slapping his hand on the kitchen table as he laughed. Until his parents glanced at him. Then he stood up straight, put on a serious face, and left the room.

The next day at school, Lizzie and Miranda made their way through the cafeteria line. Trying to fill their plates with whatever looked edible was always a challenge, but they managed to find some French fries, the always present U.F.S. (Unidentifiable Fried Stuff), and pepperoni pizza.

With her mind on their latest homework assignment, Miranda said, "I think the perfect town would be five hundred Hot Topic stores and a ten-story shopping mall."

Lizzie looked down at the sheet their

teacher had passed out and read from it. "Design a model community, including housing, hospitals, schools, and police and fire departments."

"Police and fire departments," Miranda said in a singsong voice, making fun of their teacher.

Lizzie joined in, bobbing her head from left to right as she said, "Housing, hospitals, and schools."

"We'll call it Boringville, U.S.A.," Miranda said, sitting down at their usual table. "Where do they come up with these moronic assignments?"

"The Moronic Assignment Study Guide," Lizzie explained. "It's like this thick," she said, holding her hand three feet from the ground.

As Gordo approached, he asked, "Lemme guess—that's how tall Tom Cruise is."

"Tom Cruise isn't short," Miranda said, defending the actor, who she thought was a total hottie. "He just has small bones."

"Okay, Gordo, imagine you live in a boring suburb where all the houses look alike and everybody's predictable," said Lizzie.

"I do live in a boring suburb where all the houses look alike and everyone's predictable," Gordo replied. "Thank you."

"Okay," Lizzie said. "But if you could pick any businesses you want on Main Street, what would they be?"

Gordo didn't have to think twice. Pausing with his plastic fork in midair, he said, "A bookstore containing the works of Navajo and Greek philosophers, a coffeehouse where people only discuss music and politics, a thousand-foot water slide ending in a swim-up counter where they serve free, deep-fried pizza. And Tyra Banks would be the mayor.

I've given this a lot of thought." He stabbed his fork into a piece of U.F.S.

No kidding, thought Lizzie.

Just then, Kate Sanders walked up to their table, ignoring Lizzie, which was only slightly better than sneering at her. She asked, "Hey, Gordo, do you know where the nearest Software Shack is?"

"Yeah, it's over on Collins Street," Gordo answered.

Kate tossed her long, perfect blond hair over one shoulder. "Would they have that software that designs cities and towns and stuff?"

"You mean Cyber Townmaker?" asked Gordo. "They should."

Lizzie blinked at Kate. Her former best friend wasn't just the Queen of Mean—she was the entire Royal Court. "Okay, Kate. We're supposed to do this assignment ourselves."

"Whatever," Kate replied with a sneer.

"You're supposed to use your imagination, not have some computer do it for you," said Lizzie. Then she turned to Gordo, obviously irritated, and said, "Gordo, why didn't you tell me there was a program like that?"

"Well, it costs sixty bucks," he answered.

He turned to Kate. "I don't think you can afford it," he told her.

"Hello," said Kate. "I baby-sat *twice* last week."

Kate could baby-sit? This was so unfair! Lizzie knew she could do such a better job than the snob. What did Kate know about baby-sitting? Sure, Lizzie thought, baby-sitting was probably a snap for Kate—once she learned how to tune out the crying and whining kids. Kate probably thought it was all about getting paid to talk on the phone, polish her nails, and eat whatever great food she could find in the refrigerator. Ugh!

Pulling a wad of cash from her wallet, Kate began to count out the bills. "Twenty, forty, sixty . . . Oh, look, I have more." After waving her cash in the air, and making sure Lizzie, Miranda, and Gordo were adequately awed, she walked away.

Lizzie watched her go. "Kate baby-sits?" she said. "Since when does Kate baby-sit? Why don't they just make her Queen of the World and be done with it?"

"Baby-sitting sounds like a pretty sweet gig. Why don't you do it?" asked Gordo.

Lizzie winced. "I don't baby-sit. I get baby-sat." Lizzie imagined herself trapped in a playpen, with some chubby-cheeked elderly woman shoving a stuffed bunny rabbit in her face. The thought made her want to hide under a rock, as far away from Kate Sanders and everyone else as she could get.

"I don't get it," she said. "I mean, I'm the same age as Kate. I'm as mature as she is. I'm responsible. . . ."

Later that day Lizzie pleaded with her parents. ". . . and I want to baby-sit!"

"Absolutely not," said Mr. McGuire as he sat at the kitchen table, touching up the paint job on a lawn gnome.

Lizzie was so upset, she almost stamped her foot. Of course, she realized that throwing a tantrum like a kid was not the best way to prove she was mature enough to take *care* of kids. "But Kate Sanders baby-sits."

"She does?" Mrs. McGuire asked, wondering for a second if she could see if Kate was free on Saturday.

Mr. McGuire, doing that mind-reading thing that Lizzie's parents can do with each other, shook his head *no*. So Mrs. McGuire shifted her tone of voice to neutral. "I mean, she, she does, huh?"

"Yes," Lizzie told them. "And you haven't found a sitter for tonight. And you trust me to ride the bus to school all by myself. Why can't you trust me to baby-sit?"

"Hmmm." As Mrs. McGuire carried a stack of plates and silverware from the island to the kitchen table, she tried to come up with a reason. When none came to mind, she realized Lizzie might be on to something.

i think i'm getting a nibble here.

Mrs. McGuire turned to her husband. "Maybe she has a point."

"And Miranda can help me. She watches her baby sister after school," Lizzie said. She didn't mention the fact that Miranda always complained about how gross it was to have to change her sister's dirty, smelly diapers.

Still, Mr. McGuire didn't budge. "Sweetheart, you're just not ready yet. This is a big responsibility."

"Well, you've always told me I can do anything if I set my mind to it," Lizzie said. "And I've set my mind to this. I can do it."

"We do say that, Sam," Mrs. McGuire had to admit to Mr. McGuire.

Ooh, I'm *really* getting a nibble here.

Mr. McGuire panicked. "But Matt can be quite a handful," he tried.

Mrs. McGuire turned toward the living room, where Matt was lying facedown on the couch. You might think he was asleep, except whenever a commercial came on—then he managed to point the remote at the TV and change the channel. "Matt, what would you do if Lizzie baby-sat you?"

"I dunno," Matt replied lazily, not taking his eyes off his cartoons. "Watch TV, I guess."

"Thank you for the help, pal," Mr. McGuire quipped, sarcastically. He turned back to his lawn gnome and tried to paint, but he knew Lizzie was waiting for an answer. "All right. Maybe we can give this a try."

Yes! Lizzie was so psyched! "Thanks, Dad." She gave her father a gigantic hug. "It means a lot to me that you can trust me. I'll do a great job."

CHAPTER TWO

That night, Matt sat on the sofa, playing a video game and eating popcorn. Lizzie and Miranda were on the floor, arranging empty cereal boxes and juice containers for their model community. They even had an electric train set chugging around town in a loop. By offering good public transportation, Lizzie planned to create a more environmentally friendly city, where people didn't need to depend on cars.

"Okay," Lizzie said. "The Coco Drops will be city hall."

Miranda grabbed a handful of the cereal and ate some. "I just ate the mayor," she said.

Just then, Mr. and Mrs. McGuire came downstairs, all dressed up for their big date. Mr. McGuire's conservative dark suit didn't go so well with the freaked-out look on his face. "Lizzie," he said. "I added some numbers to the emergency phone list. Also, I moved all the cleaners out from under the kitchen sink. And whatever you do, do not open the door for anybody."

"And I won't follow the trail of bread crumbs to the gingerbread witch's house," Lizzie said. "Dad, don't worry."

Mr. McGuire exhaled, loudly. He couldn't even pretend that he wasn't nervous. His heart was racing, his palms were sweating, and his feet felt like they were glued to the floor.

He would have done anything to stay at home, but Mrs. McGuire had insisted they go out.

The doorbell rang and Mrs. McGuire answered it. "Hey, Gordo," she said.

"Hi, Mrs. McGuire." Gordo slipped into the house. "My parents said I could come over if that's okay with you."

"Oh, sure," said Mrs. McGuire. "But Lizzie and Miranda are baby-sitting Matt, so I don't know how much fun you're gonna have."

"Oh, I know. I'm not about fun. I'm about the green," said Gordo.

Mrs. McGuire was thoroughly confused and turned to her daughter for a translation. "Lizzie?"

"Money," Lizzie answered.

Sinking down on the couch, Gordo grabbed a bowl of popcorn from Miranda's lap. "I'm gonna earn my money indoors," he said. "Sitting on a sofa, eating someone else's popcorn."

"Hey, that's mine." Miranda grabbed for the bowl, but Gordo held it out of her reach.

"Lizzie, Matt's bedtime is nine o'clock," Mr. McGuire said.

"Yes, Dad, I know." Lizzie stood up and pushed her parents toward the front door. "Dad, listen, everything's under control. I've got it all handled, okay?"

Mr. McGuire said, "Okay, now both our cell phones are charged. And we're trusting you, Lizzie."

"Whoa," said Lizzie. "Can I hear that again?"

"Both of our cell phones are charged?" he asked.

"No, no, no," said Lizzie. "The other part."

"We're trusting you," Mr. McGuire repeated.

"Yeah, that," Lizzie said, happily.

Ta-da! After all these years—trust!

"Thanks, Dad." Lizzie watched her parents leave, thinking, I'm alone in the house, with trust—this is way cool.

Wow. For the first time in my life, i'm in charge. i'm the ranking adult in the house. i'm Queen of the World!

"Alone, at last," Lizzie mused.

"I don't see why you have to muscle in on baby-sitting, Gordo. This is how *we* make money," Miranda complained.

"Why should girls have a monopoly on baby-sitting?" Gordo asked.

"Because boys have a monopoly on burping the Pledge of Allegiance," Miranda answered. "We deserve some kind of monopoly."

"Hey, I love that game," said Matt. "I wanna be the race car."

"Tough luck," Lizzie told him. "You're gonna watch *Willie Wonka.*"

"I've seen that ten times," Matt protested. "I wanna be the race car!"

"Well, we've got homework," said Lizzie. "If you'll be patient, we'll maybe play later, okay?"

"All right." Matt sighed.

Lizzie smiled at her friends. She handled that well. She and Gordo high-fived, and Lizzie realized that this baby-sitting thing was a piece of cake—with extra chocolate frosting on top!

Two minutes later, Matt was jumping up and down on the sofa, like he was the Energizer bunny on overload. "Race car! Race car! Race car! Race car! Race car!" He chanted as he bounced so hard and fast that Lizzie couldn't believe the couch springs didn't pop right through the fabric.

Lizzie's, Gordo's, and Miranda's heads moved up and down as they watched Matt bouncing. It was like they were keeping their eyes on a ball in some kind of weird, vertical Ping-Pong tournament.

"Anyone got any ideas?" Lizzie asked.

Miranda and Gordo shook their heads.

"Sorry," Miranda said.

"I got nothing," Gordo added.

Matt jumped off the couch and zipped around the room. "Race car! Race car!" he shouted, leaping back onto the couch. It was almost as bad as the maple syrup night!

Meanwhile Mr. and Mrs. McGuire arrived at Panda Garden, their favorite Chinese restaurant. The hostess, Mrs. Shin, greeted them with a warm smile and showed them to their table. "Here you go, Mr. and Mrs. McGuire. Your regular table."

"Thank you, Mrs. Shin." Mr. McGuire settled down into his seat.

"Haven't seen you since the Year of the Tiger," said Mrs. Shin.

"Yeah, well, it's really hard to get a reliable baby-sitter," Mr. McGuire explained.

"Well, glad to have you back," Mrs. Shin said. "I'll be back with some wontons."

Mrs. McGuire smiled and said, "Thank you."

Mr. McGuire picked up one corner of his bright orange napkin and unfolded it. He tried not to think of what was going on back at the house, but a list of possible disasters ran through his mind: fires and floods, break-ins and broken limbs. . . . He strained to listen for fire, ambulance, or police sirens outside.

Mrs. McGuire said, "Sam, would you please relax. It's one night out. Lizzie can handle it. I mean that. Everything's gonna be fine."

Mr. McGuire picked up his wooden chopsticks, which were joined at the top, separated them, and started rubbing them together to get rid of any splinters.

Back at the McGuire house, Lizzie was on her hands and knees, furiously scrubbing at a new purple stain on the rug. Matt dabbed at a second, matching purple stain on his shirt.

"This had better come out of the carpet, Matt," said Lizzie, annoyed that the more she tried to clean, the bigger the stain became.

She glared at Miranda. "What did you give him grape juice for? I told you ginger ale. Ginger ale isn't purple."

"Grape juice was the only thing that would shut him up," said Miranda. "He won't do a thing you say."

"Matt, go upstairs," Lizzie said. "Change your shirt and get cleaned up. Now."

"No," Matt said, simply.

"See?" Miranda said. She wanted to say, "I told you so," but knew it would upset Lizzie too much. Baby-sitting her sister was *never* this hard. Of course, Miranda's little sister was still too young to talk back.

"Zip it," Lizzie said to Miranda.

"Why should I? *He* won't," Miranda pointed out, oh-so-helpfully.

Lizzie was feeling desperate. "Matt, starting right now, you do everything I tell you, or I'll tell Mom and Dad."

"Nuh-uh," Matt said with a satisfied little grin. "You want Mom and Dad to think you're a good baby-sitter, so you're gonna say things went great."

"Then I'll squash you like a bug instead," Lizzie said.

"Then I'll tell Mom and Dad." Matt sat down on the couch and made himself comfortable. He had his sister just where he wanted her! "Face it—I'm in charge here."

Lizzie raised her voice. "No, *I* am in charge here."

Gordo stepped in and said, "Matt, what do you say we go upstairs and find you a clean shirt?"

"Okay," Matt said.

"How come he does what you say?" Lizzie asked, totally outraged.

"I'm an older man," Gordo explained. "He's impressed by me."

"Well, I'm in charge here, and he's supposed to do what *I* say, not what you say," Lizzie replied.

"Who cares who says to do it?" Gordo asked. "He needs a new shirt. He's as sticky as the floor of a movie theater."

Lizzie was about to protest when she saw Matt inching dangerously close to the wall. "Matt, don't lean there!" she said. Too late.

Matt tried to move away from the wall, but couldn't. "I'm stuck," he said.

"Matt?" Lizzie grabbed onto one of Matt's arms and pulled. She was horrified to discover that he was, in fact, stuck to the wall like a gnat to flypaper.

CHAPTER THREE

Whoever said that tea was supposed to calm your nerves never met a man who just let his daughter baby-sit for the first time. Mr. McGuire took a sip from his small cup of tea. Nope, not relaxing at all. Not one bit. He wondered what was going on back at the house, and if he had remembered to lock all the doors, and to tell Lizzie and Matt not to play with matches.

"Gosh, it is so nice to eat out, just the two of us for a change," Mrs. McGuire said, calmly.

"Yep, nice." Mr. McGuire rubbed his chopsticks together, not realizing he'd been doing just that for the past ten minutes.

"Sam, you're turning your chopsticks into toothpicks. Want to settle down? You're fidgeting," Mrs. McGuire observed.

"No, I'm not," said Mr. McGuire, as he fidgeted away.

Mrs. McGuire shot him a look that asked, "Who are you trying to fool?"

"Okay, look," said Mr. McGuire. "I just think it was a mistake leaving Lizzie in charge."

Mrs. McGuire said, "But she never gets in trouble at school. She gets there and back all by herself, and she's the only one in the house who knows how to make the picture-in-picture work."

"Yeah, but she sleeps until noon on the weekends. She uses the picture-in-picture to watch MTV and cartoons at the same time." When his wife didn't say anything Mr. McGuire started to stand up. "I gotta go check on her."

"No, you do not," Mrs. McGuire said, in her sternest voice that was usually reserved for talking to Matt and Lizzie. "Do you know how much it meant to her that you trusted her?"

"Okay, I tell you what," Mr. McGuire said. "I'll just sneak in, look in a window. She'll never even know I'm there."

Mrs. McGuire sighed. "Okay. If I let you go, do you promise me that you will come right back here and eat your meal in peace?"

"Yeah." Mr. McGuire nodded, flashing his wife a grin.

"Okay," Mrs. McGuire said with a sigh.

As Mr. McGuire bolted up out of his seat and ran for the front door, Mrs. McGuire said, "But she'd better not know you're there. I swear she will never forgive you."

"Okay," Mr. McGuire called, already halfway out the door.

"And I won't forgive you until she does," Mrs. McGuire added.

Lizzie scrubbed furiously at the grape juice stain. Matt's old shirt was stuck to the wall, but at least he'd gone upstairs to change into a clean one.

Hearing a strange buzzing noise, Lizzie looked up to see Matt with the vacuum cleaner. The day's newspaper was stuck to the hose. "Look, it holds up newspapers," he said.

"Cut it out, Matt," Lizzie said.

Ignoring her, Matt looked for something else to suction. He came back a minute later. "Look, it holds up Mom's cat calendar."

"Gordo, can you tell him to quit that?" Lizzie yelled.

"You're in charge—you do it," Gordo said, not taking his eyes off the television.

"Could you at least help?" Lizzie cried. "You didn't come over here to watch TV on the couch."

Realizing that Lizzie had a good point, Gordo stood up and turned the TV off. "All right," he said. "I'll watch TV in your room."

"Miranda, get me more paper towels," Lizzie said.

"Pass," Miranda replied. "I'm building a ten-story shopping mall for Mirandaville."

"Well, Mirandaville doesn't need a ten-story shopping mall," said Lizzie, somewhat hysterically. "We need a hospital."

"Fine." Miranda shrugged. "I'll go drink some orange juice and make a mall out of that!"

"Fine! Nobody help me do anything!" Lizzie yelled.

Matt walked over to Lizzie with the vacuum. "Look, it holds up Dad's briefcase."

"I'll just handle everything myself!" Lizzie yelled.

Suddenly, the vacuum motor made a funny noise and burned out. Half a second later, all of the electricity cut out, plunging everyone into darkness.

"Um, I may need a little help here," said Lizzie, looking around the room.

i hate it when Dad's right.

Matt found a flashlight, held it up to his chin, and turned it on. With only his face lit up he said in a voice trembling with fear, "Lizzie, I'm scared!" A second later, he said in a deep and scratchy voice, "Look at me, I'm a monster." Next he whispered, "I see dead people."

"Cut it out, Matt," Lizzie warned.

Meanwhile, Mr. McGuire crept up to the house slowly, feeling like a burglar from an old movie. Since all the curtains were drawn, he couldn't see inside. And because they were so thick, he couldn't see that the lights were off. But looking up, he noticed the transom over the door. A clear window! If only it weren't so high up . . .

In the kitchen, Lizzie lit some of her new candles.

"Whew, that stinks!" Matt said, holding his nose in disgust.

"It's vanilla," Lizzie said, through clenched teeth. "It's soothing."

Miranda raised her eyebrows. "Works like a charm," she said, sarcastically.

Gordo walked into the kitchen and waved his hand in front of his face. "Whoa! Who's burning garbage?"

"I'm trying to get some light in here," Lizzie said. "If you're not going to help me, you could at least hush up."

"Don't tell us to 'hush up,'" Miranda said. "We're not babies."

"You're *acting* like babies," Lizzie replied.

"It's a shame there isn't a decent baby-sitter around," Gordo said.

Ouch! Lizzie looked around the house. She took in the stained rug, the shorted-out electricity, and Matt's sticky shirt. "I'm sure there'll be a decent baby-sitter around next time," she said. "'Cause I obviously can't handle it."

* * *

Back outside, Mr. McGuire climbed onto the seat of a chair, and tried to peek in the window, but found he still wasn't tall enough. He stepped to the back of the chair, and tried to pull his body up with his fingertips. He was almost there, when the chair gave out from under him, and he tumbled to the ground, slamming his neck into the pointy little hat of the lawn gnome. "Ahh!" he shouted.

Lizzie jumped up and aimed her flashlight toward the back door. "What was that?"

"Do you think it's a burglar?" asked Miranda.

"Naw," said Gordo. "It's probably just a raccoon. They root around in the trash and stuff."

"Yeah, it's probably just a raccoon. Let's make noises, just in case," said Lizzie.

She rang a bell as Miranda belted out the

only tune she could think of: "My country 'tis of thee, sweet land of liberty, of thee I sing." She was way off-key, and if anything was going to spook a burglar, her singing was *so* it.

"I'm gonna go and flip the circuit breakers, so we can play some loud music," said Gordo. Glancing at Miranda, he added, "Real music."

Mr. McGuire sat on the ground, coughing and rubbing his neck, which seriously ached. As he tried to remember what had happened, his cell phone began to ring. "Hello?" he croaked.

"What is taking so long?" asked Mrs. McGuire. She was still at Panda Garden, staring at the tableful of delicious but now cold food.

"All the curtains are shut," Mr. McGuire explained hoarsely, between coughs. "And I can't see in the house."

"Okay, just get in there, pretend you forgot your wallet, make sure they're okay, and get right out," said Mrs. McGuire.

"Gotcha."

"What's wrong with your voice?"

"Uh, mmm, lawn gnome," Mr. McGuire replied. As soon as he hung up, the lights in the house went on.

Miranda turned on the stereo, blasting pop music. Lizzie stopped ringing her bell as Gordo entered the room.

"You think it went away, right?" she asked.

"A raccoon wouldn't stick around through this racket," Gordo said.

Suddenly, the doorknob started to turn. The door slowly creaked open, but only by a couple of inches, since the chain was fastened.

Lizzie screamed.

"A raccoon wouldn't do that, either," Miranda observed.

"Kids, open up—it's me," Mr. McGuire croaked.

Code Blue! Seeing the outline of a man's body and an actual hand groping around inside, Lizzie shouted, "It *is* a burglar!" She ran to her little brother and gave him a hug. "Matt!"

"Lizzie!" Matt exclaimed, truly scared.

Meanwhile, Mr. McGuire forced his hand further through the crack in the door and tried to unlatch the chain.

Lizzie knew she had to do something. She was the baby-sitter, after all. Everyone's safety depended on her. Taking a deep breath, she yelled, "AAAGGHH!" and charged at the door. Lizzie slammed into it with all her might, crushing what she thought was a stranger's wrist.

Crunch! A searing pain shot up Mr. McGuire's arm and he screamed in agony. "Aarrgh!" He pulled his hand free and checked for damage.

Meanwhile, Lizzie stood with her back pressed against the door.

"That ought to drive him away," said Gordo.

Matt clung to his sister. "Lizzie, I'm really scared."

"It's okay. I'm not gonna let anything happen to you, okay?" said Lizzie. "We're gonna call the police."

Matt's and Lizzie's frightened eyes locked. Lizzie thought, You may be an annoying twerp with hair that looks like the back of a porcupine, but you're still my brother. Matt thought, Although you're totally bossy and you finished all the Froot Loops last week, you're really not so bad.

* * *

Meanwhile, Mr. McGuire was stumbling around outside. Water! he thought. Water will soothe my aching pain. He plunged his hand into the kiddie pool, breathed in deeply, and tried to come up with a new plan to break into his own house.

CHAPTER FOUR

Back at Panda Garden, Mrs. Shin sat next to Mrs. McGuire and they both stared at the tableful of delicious, untouched food.

"You know," said Mrs. Shin, "I have a cousin. Knows how to treat a lady."

"Mrs. Shin, my husband didn't leave me," said Mrs. McGuire. "I mean, he left me but he didn't leave me."

Mrs. Shin shook her head. "Aw, yeah, you're keeping your chin up." She shoveled some steamed dumplings onto Mrs. McGuire's plate. "Brave, brave, little soldier girl."

Mr. McGuire shook his hand dry, pulled out his cell phone, and dialed the house.

Lizzie picked up on the first ring. "Hello?"

"It's me," her dad croaked into the phone with his hoarse voice.

Lizzie's eyes widened in terror. "It's him!"

"I'm at home!" Mr. McGuire tried to explain.

But Lizzie misheard him. "He knows we're alone!" she cried.

Mr. McGuire dragged his injured body to the door. "Come on, kids," he said as he jiggled the doorknob one more time.

Lizzie screamed, and then Miranda, Gordo, and Matt joined her.

Matt even slapped his hands to his cheeks and struck a perfect *Home Alone* pose.

"It's worse!" said Miranda in a shaking voice. "He's at the door."

"Gordo, Miranda, get the train-transformer," Lizzie said, thinking fast.

Mr. McGuire continued to shake the knob and pound on the door.

Back inside, Gordo wrapped the lead wires from the Mirandaville train set around the doorknob. When everything was secure, he signaled to Lizzie, who kneeled by a power outlet with the transformer cord in her hand.

"Now!" said Gordo.

It was action time! As Lizzie plugged the cord in, Matt flipped the lever and sparks leaped from the doorknob.

Mr. McGuire, who was holding the door-knob, received a huge jolt of juice. He shook all over and tried to let go, but it felt like his hand was superglued to the door. He was finally able to pull away from the evil grip of the doorknob. But like a tug-of-war where the other team lets go of the rope midgame, he flew backward, tripped over the gnome, and landed right in the kiddie pool.

"Lawn gnome," he moaned indignantly.

Back at the McGuire house, everyone was still in a state of panic. They raced around, checking the doors and windows to make sure everything was secure.

Mr. McGuire knew none of this, and he'd had enough. He found his hacksaw in the garage and limped back toward the door.

As Matt and Lizzie double-locked the French doors in back, Matt said, "You can baby-sit for me anytime."

"Let's get through tonight first, okay?" Lizzie responded.

Suddenly, she heard a sawing sound. Looking toward the back door, she saw the top half of the hacksaw moving back and forth, eating its way through the chain.

Lizzie screamed. Then she came up with a plan. "Gordo, get the train. Miranda, fill the paint can with flour, now!" To Matt she shouted, "Come on, come on!"

Mr. McGuire sawed away, pleased that he was actually making progress.

Miranda looped a long piece of twine through the handle of the paint can full of flour, as Gordo lashed a paring knife to the swinging arm of the crossing gate. Once Matt wolfed down a grape Popsicle, Lizzie took the stick and taped it to the train transformer lever, and placed it by the door. Lizzie and her friends assembled these various parts into the perfect booby trap! They weren't going to let this maniac get into the house without pounding him hard!

* * *

The intruder was still working the lock, and laughing maniacally with frustration. Lizzie darted into the kitchen, to join everyone else who was hiding behind the counter.

"That was some fast Popsicle eating, Matt," Lizzie said.

Matt's mouth was ringed with purple. "Thanks," he said, raising his fingers to his forehead. "I have major brain-freeze."

Once Mr. McGuire cut through the chain, he turned the doorknob, thinking, Victory, finally!

As the door opened, the Popsicle stick pushed the train transformer to full speed.

The locomotive sped across the kitchen floor with a long piece of twine tied to it. The twine was threaded through a hook in the ceiling, and the other end was fastened to a paint can. . . . And as the train chugged down the track, it pulled the paint can higher and higher!

Then, suddenly . . .

"Dad?" asked Matt, surprised that the burglar was his own father.

But before Matt could stop it, the train reached the end of the track, where a knife attached to the crossing gate arm swung down. The twine was severed in an instant. It released the paint can, which came swinging down from the ceiling to hit Mr. McGuire in the stomach!

"Youch!" he yelped as he doubled over and was sent flying back outside.

Lizzie, Matt, Gordo, and Miranda watched from behind the counter, completely stunned.

"You guys have to trust me," said Gordo. "You have no idea how much that hurts."

"Omigosh! Your poor father," said Miranda.

They walked across the kitchen and peeked out into the backyard, where Mr. McGuire was writhing in pain. He kicked the lawn gnome hard, smashing his toe in the process. Angry, in pain, feeling pathetic, and soaked to the bone, he jumped around.

Matt leaned against the door frame and said, "We are so in trouble."

"He was supposed to trust me," Lizzie said, in a hurt voice.

"Well," Gordo said. "If he was spying on you—and I admit it does look like he was—I'd think he suffered enough."

Just then, a police car with flashing red lights pulled into the driveway. A police siren blasted, and then a voice came over the loud-speaker: "Sir, please put your hands on your head and don't move."

Moments later, two cops led the intruder to the house. "I'm telling you, I live here," he was saying. "My kids are inside."

Unsure of whether or not to believe this wet and clearly disturbed man, one of the officers knocked on the door.

Mr. McGuire explained, "I just came home to check on them."

Lizzie opened the door, wearing her best "I'm innocent, didn't do it, don't know what's going on" expression. "Yes?" she asked.

"Hello, young lady," said the policeman. "Is this man your father?"

Lizzie blinked and refused to even look at her dad when she said, "I don't know why my father would be sneaking around in the bushes late at night. Maybe that means he doesn't trust me." She shrugged one shoulder, innocently.

"Lizzie!" Mr. McGuire muttered through clenched teeth.

Lizzie rolled her eyes to the sky. "That's my father," she told the officers.

"Good night, sir," said one cop. "And by the way, your lawn gnome is broken."

Later that night, wrapped in a bright blue towel, Mr. McGuire slumped over the kitchen counter. Mrs. McGuire rubbed his back.

"You were supposed to trust me," Lizzie reminded her dad.

Mrs. McGuire nodded. "Yes, we were. And we didn't stick to our word, and we were wrong."

They're admitting they were wrong? Call the news crews. Film at eleven.

Mr. McGuire sat up and tried to explain

himself. "It's not that I don't trust you, sweet-heart. I guess I still just think of you as the six-year-old girl that used to need me to chase the monsters out of her closet. I guess I have to get used to the fact that you're not that little girl anymore. You're becoming a young lady, and I have to let you act like one."

Lizzie's anger melted away with each word of her dad's sappy-but-sweet explanation. Hmm, now how can I milk this? she wondered. "So, I can go on a real date?" she asked.

"No," said Mr. McGuire.

"Will you teach me how to drive?" she tried.

"No," said Mr. McGuire.

"Can I dye my hair?"

No, again.

"Well, what can I do?" she asked.

"You can baby-sit Matt next Saturday night," Mrs. McGuire said.

"Yeah," said Mr. McGuire, knowing that next time he'd stay far away from the house when Lizzie was in charge. He had a feeling he'd be sorry if he didn't!

So, the more responsibility i ask for, the more responsibility i get stuck with. That stinks. i think.

Okay, it wasn't as good as driving, or dating, or dyeing her hair, but baby-sitting was *something*. And it felt pretty great.

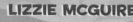

LIZZIE MCGUIRE
2-IN-1

Say Cheese!

it's Picture Day, and Lizzie's parents have pressured her into wearing the dorky unicorn sweater her grandmother gave her. Not exactly the fashion statement Lizzie was going for! Lizzie really doesn't want to be remembered in the yearbook as the Girl in the Unicorn Sweater. Will she be able to come up with a plan to find a new outfit . . . before three o'clock?

The name's Bond . . . Matt Bond.

Lizzie can't believe it—her crush boy Ethan Craft actually wants to have lunch with her! Not only that, but she'll also get to meet his new friend, a mysterious kid who's made a movie with Steven Spielberg, skipped three grades, and taught Britney Spears how to dance. Talk about instant popularity! But wait . . . the new kid looks awfully familiar! it couldn't be . . . could it?

Visit Lizzie every day at DisneyChannel.co.uk

Get ready for a double dose of Lizzie!

Love-bugged!

Gordo's always been there for Lizzie—a true best friend. But when he starts secretly dating pretty Brooke Baker, he makes up stupid excuses to ditch Lizzie. Gordo's a frog, not a prince. So Brooke must be two-timing him. Lizzie advises Gordo to dump Brooke before he gets hurt. But is Lizzie truly worried about Gordo's feelings—or is she just trying to protect her own?

Supermodel . . . or supermuddle?

When Lizzie goes to a local modeling tryout, she gets a contract with *Teen Attitude* magazine. Totally cool, right? Wrong. Everyone keeps staring and even her two best friends have joined the suck-up bandwagon. Yuck! Too weird for words. Lizzie wants her old life back. But how does a girl get out of a modeling contract? One thing's for sure—it won't be pretty!

Visit Lizzie every day at DisneyChannel.co.uk

Get ready for a double dose of Lizzie!

GET INSIDE HER HEAD

Lizzie McGUiRE

A Disney Channel Original Series

Weekends

Watch it on

Visit Lizzie every day at DisneyChannel.co.uk